Emil
and the Sneaky Rat

BY **ASTRID LINDGREN**

ILLUSTRATED BY **MINI GREY**

TRANSLATED BY **SUSAN BEARD**

OXFORD
UNIVERSITY PRESS

THE WORLD OF
ASTRID LINDGREN

BOOKS BY ASTRID LINDGREN
ILLUSTRATED BY MINI GREY

Pippi Longstocking

Pippi Longstocking Goes Aboard

Pippi Longstocking in the South Seas

Emil's Clever Pig

Emil and the Great Escape

Emil and the Sneaky Rat

Lotta Says 'No!'

Lotta Makes a Mess

Karlsson Flies Again

Karlsson on the Roof

The World's Best Karlsson

The Children of Noisy Village

Nothing but Fun in Noisy Village

Happy Times in Noisy Village

CONTENTS

Emil

and the Sneaky Rat

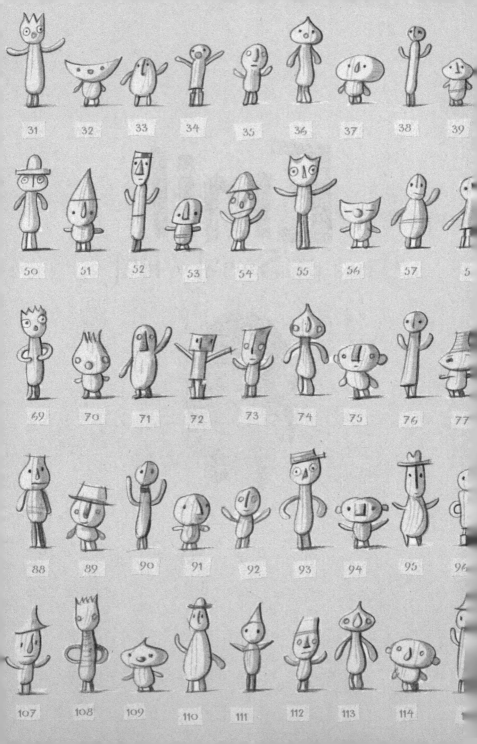

31   32   33   34   35   36   37   38   39

50   51   52   53   54   55   56   57   5

69   70   71   72   73   74   75   76   77

88   89   90   91   92   93   94   95   96

107   108   109   110   111   112   113   114

Have you ever heard of Emil from Lönneberga, the little boy who lived on Katthult Farm in Lönneberga, in a place called Småland in Sweden? You haven't? Well, I can tell you, in Lönneberga there wasn't a single person who hadn't heard all about Katthult Farm's dreadful little boy, that Emil, who got up to more mischief than there were days in the year and who scared the people of Lönneberga so much that they wanted to pack him off to America. Yes, they really did. The people of Lönneberga collected money, tied it up in a bundle, and took it to Emil's mother and said:

'There might be enough here for you to send Emil to America.'

3

They thought it would be much more peaceful in Lönneberga if Emil wasn't around, and they were right, of course, but it made Emil's mother so furious she threw the money back at them and it flew all over Lönneberga.

'Emil is a lovely little boy,' she said. 'We love him just as he is.'

And Lina, the girl who was the maid at Katthult, she said:

'We ought to think about those Americans, too. They haven't done us any harm so why should we dump Emil on them?'

That's when Emil's mother looked at Lina long and hard, so that Lina understood she had said something stupid. She started to stutter, wanting to make it better:

'Yes but,' she said, 'it says in the *Vimmerby Times* all about that terrible earthquake over there in Amayrica . . . and, I mean, well, it would be too much if, on top of all that, Emil . . .'

'Quiet, Lina,' said Emil's mother. 'Get off to the barn and do the milking, that's the only thing you understand.'

So Lina picked up her milking stool and strode off to the barn. She sat down and started milking so fast that the milk splashed in all directions. She always worked best when she was a bit angry, which is why this time she did the milking faster than usual, all the time muttering quietly to herself:

'There's no justice! Why have those Americans

got to have all the problems, anyway? Oh, I'd like to change places with them. I think I might just write them a letter saying, here you are, here's Emil. Now send us that earthquake!'

What a show-off she was, that Lina, thinking she could write a letter to America when she couldn't even write so that the people in Småland could understand! No, if anyone was going to write to America it ought to be Emil's mother. She was very good at writing. She wrote down all Emil's mischief in a notebook with a blue cover, which she kept in the bureau drawer.

'What's the point of doing that?' said Emil's father. 'With all the pranks that child gets up to you'll be using up all our ink, have you thought of that?'

That didn't bother Emil's mother. She wrote down all Emil's mischief so that when Emil grew up he would know exactly what he had got up to when he was little. Because then, she thought, he would understand why his mother's hair had turned grey and then perhaps he would love her even though she had a headful of grey hair, which she had got because of him.

Now you mustn't think that Emil was nasty—oh no, his mother was absolutely right when she said that he was a lovely little boy. Just like an angel he looked, with his fluffy blond hair and his innocent blue eyes. Of course Emil was a kind boy, and his mother wasn't unfair, so she wrote exactly that in the blue notebook.

'*Yesterday Emil was well behayved,*' she wrote in her book on the twenty-seventh of July. '*He did not get up too a single bad thing all day which was becos he had a high tempreture and could not qwite manage too.*'

But the very next day, the twenty-eighth of July, Emil's temperature was down far enough for his mischief to fill several pages in the notebook, because he was as strong as a little ox, that boy, and as long as he was well he could get into all sorts of trouble.

'I've never known a child like him,' said Lina.

You might have understood by now that Lina didn't really like Emil. She preferred Ida, Emil's little sister, who was a good, obedient child. But Alfred, the farmhand at Katthult, he liked Emil, nobody really knows why, and Emil liked Alfred. They had fun together when Alfred wasn't working and Alfred taught Emil all sorts of useful things, such as how you harness a horse and how to catch pike when you go fishing and how you chew tobacco—well, that isn't exactly useful, as I'm sure you know, which is why Emil only tried it once. But try it he did, because he wanted to know everything Alfred knew and be able to do everything that Alfred did.

Alfred had carved a wooden rifle for Emil—wasn't that kind of him? That wooden rifle was Emil's most treasured possession. His second most treasured possession was a scruffy little cap that his father had bought for him once when he was in town and can't have been thinking straight.

'I like me gun and me hat,' Emil used to say, and every single night when he went to bed he had his gun and his hat in bed beside him.

Now, do you remember who lived at Katthult Farm? There was Emil's father who was called Anton, Emil's mother who was called Alma, Emil's sister who was called Ida, the farmhand who was called Alfred, the maid who was called

Lina, and then there was Emil, who was called Emil. Oh, and Krösa-Maja, of course, we mustn't forget her. She was a scrawny little old woman who lived in a farm worker's cottage up in the forest, but she was always running backwards and forwards to Katthult to help with the laundry and sausage-stuffing and things like that, and to scare Emil and Ida half to death with her terrible stories about ghosts and murderers and robbers and other nice things which Krösa-Maja knew all about.

But perhaps now you would like to hear about some of the trouble Emil got into? He got into trouble every single day, except when he had a temperature, so we could easily pick any old day and he would have got up to something. Well then, why not take the very day we were talking about, the twenty-eighth of July?

SATURDAY
THE TWENTY-EIGHTH
OF JULY:

Emil and the Sneaky Rat

In the kitchen on Katthult Farm was an old sofa and that was where Lina slept. It was made of wood and painted blue and when you lifted the seat, there underneath was a mattress. In those days, when this story happened, Småland was full of kitchen sofa beds with maids sleeping in them on knobbly mattresses, with flies buzzing all around, so why should it be any different on Katthult Farm? Lina slept so soundly in her sofa bed that nothing could wake her up before half past four in the morning, when the alarm clock went off and she had to get up to do the milking.

As soon as there was no Lina in the kitchen,

Emil's father used to come creeping in to drink his morning coffee in peace and quiet, before Emil woke up. He thought it was lovely to sit there at the big table all alone, not having to watch out for that Emil, listening to the birds singing and the hens cackling outside, slurping his coffee, tipping his chair back and feeling the lovely smooth floorboards under his feet which Lina had scrubbed until they were white . . . no, you know what I mean, it was the *floorboards* she had scrubbed, not Emil's father's feet, although perhaps they could have done with a scrub, what do I know? Emil's father went around barefoot in the morning, but not only because he liked the feel of it.

'We might as well save on shoe leather,' he said to Emil's mother, who was very hard-working and didn't at all like going barefoot. 'The way you're wearing out shoes, we have to keep on buying new ones every ten years.'

'Exactly,' said Emil's mother, and that was the end of that conversation.

I've already told you that nothing could wake Lina before the alarm clock went off but one morning she was woken up by something else. It was the twenty-seventh of July, the day Emil had a temperature, and it was only four o'clock in the morning when Lina was woken up by a big rat scampering right across her face—can you imagine anything so awful? She shot out of bed with a scream and grabbed hold of a log from beside the stove, but by that time the rat had disappeared down a hole next to the box where they kept the logs.

Emil's father got all worked up when he heard about the rat.

'That's a proper nice thing to happen!' said Emil's father. 'Rats in the kitchen! They'll be eating up all our bread and bacon!'

'And *me*,' said Lina.

'*And* our bread and bacon,' said Emil's father. 'That cat's coming into the kitchen tonight.'

Emil heard about the rat and even though he had a temperature he started plotting right away how to catch it, if the plan with the cat didn't work out.

At ten o'clock that night, on the twenty-seventh of July, Emil's temperature was down to normal and he wanted to get back into action. At that hour Katthult Farm was fast asleep: Emil's mother, Emil's father, and little Ida in the bedroom next to the kitchen, Lina in her sofa bed, and Alfred in the farmhand's cottage by the tool shed. Pigs and hens were sleeping in the pigsty and in the hen-house, and cows, horses, and sheep were asleep in the green meadows. But in the kitchen the cat sat wide awake, longing to be back in the barn where there were more rats. Emil was wide awake, too, and he came tiptoeing into the kitchen from his own bed in the bedroom.

'Poor Monty, are you here?' he said, when he saw the cat's eyes shining over by the kitchen door.

'Miaow,' said Monty and because Emil loved animals so much, he let Monty out.

Of course, he understood that the rat had to be caught, but now that the cat had gone it would have to be done some other way. And that's why Emil found a mousetrap, set it with a tasty piece of bacon and placed it right beside the hole next to the log box. But then he stopped to think. If the rat saw the mousetrap as soon as it stuck its whiskers out of the hole, it would get suspicious and not go anywhere near the trap. It would be better, thought Emil, if it could sneak around the kitchen in peace and quiet for a while and then surprise, surprise, come across the trap

when it was least expecting it.

For a while he considered putting the trap on Lina's face, because that was where the rat usually ran about, but he was afraid Lina would wake up and spoil everything. No, it would have to be somewhere else. Why not under the table? That's exactly where a rat ought to go scuttling around looking for dropped bread crumbs— well, not under Emil's father's seat, of course. It wouldn't find many crumbs there.

'Wait a minute!' said Emil, stopping suddenly in the middle of the kitchen floor. 'Think if the rat goes there and doesn't find any bread crumbs and starts chewing on Pappa's big toe instead?'

Well, Emil was not going to let *that* happen, which is why he put the mousetrap under the table just where his father usually put his feet. Then he crept off to bed, very pleased with himself.

He didn't wake up again until it was a bright and sunny morning outside, and it was the loud yelling coming from the kitchen that woke him.

They must be shouting because they're happy the rat's been caught, thought Emil, but the very next second his mother came dashing in. She yanked him up out of bed, hissing in his ear:

'Quick, out to the tool shed with you, before your father gets his toe out of that mousetrap, or it'll be the end of you!' And she grabbed Emil by the hand and charged off with him to the tool shed, just as he was, dressed only in his nightshirt. This was not the time to get dressed, exactly.

'Not without my gun and my cap!' cried Emil. He grabbed his wooden gun and his blue cap and ran straight to the tool shed, so fast that his nightshirt flapped about behind him. That was where he had to sit when he had been up to his tricks.

Emil's mother bolted the door on the outside, so that Emil would not be able to get out, and Emil bolted it from the inside, so that his father would not be able to get in, which was very wise and very considerate of both of them. Emil's mother thought it was best if Emil and his father didn't meet for a few hours. That's what Emil thought, too, which is why he made extra sure the bolt was in place before he sat down calmly on the chopping block and started to carve one of his funny little wooden figures. He did that every time he was locked in the tool shed after some mischief or other and he had already managed to carve ninety-seven. They stood all lined up in a neat row on a shelf and it made Emil happy to look at them, especially when he thought about how he would soon have one hundred. That would really be something to celebrate.

'Then I'll have a party in the tool shed, but I'll only invite Alfred,' he decided, as he sat there holding his penknife. In the distance he heard the racket his father was making, but after a while it died down. Then he heard a different kind of sound instead, more like screaming, and Emil wondered anxiously what was up with his mother. But then he remembered that today was the day the pig was going to be slaughtered. She was the one who was screaming. Poor thing, the twenty-eighth of July was not a very nice day for her! He wasn't the only one not enjoying the day. At midday Emil was let out and when he came into the kitchen Ida ran up to him, full of joy.

'We're having black pudding dumplings for

dinner!' she said.

Now, perhaps you don't know what black pudding dumplings are? They are big, black lumps with a piece of fatty bacon inside. They taste like black pudding, but different and much nicer. You make black pudding dumplings from blood, just like you make black pudding from blood and, of course, now that a pig had been slaughtered on Katthult Farm, Emil's mother was going to use the blood to make black pudding dumplings. She had stirred the mixture together in a big earthenware bowl which was now standing on the table, and the large iron pot was full of boiling water on the stove. There would be enough black pudding dumplings to keep everybody happy.

'I'm going to eat eighteen,' said Ida proudly, even though she was a spindly little thing who could just about manage a half.

'Pappa won't let you,' said Emil. 'Where is he, anyway?'

'He's lying down, having a rest,' said Ida.

Emil leaned out of the kitchen window. Sure enough, on the grass underneath the window, there lay Emil's father, with his big straw hat over his face, having his usual after-dinner nap. He didn't normally have it *before* dinner but afterwards, of course, but probably he was especially tired today. Perhaps that's what happens when you start the day in a mousetrap.

Emil noticed that his father was wearing only one shoe. At first he hoped it was just because his father was being economical and didn't want to wear out more than one shoe at a time, but then he saw the blood-stained bandage tied around the big toe of his father's left foot, and then he understood. His father's toe hurt so much he couldn't bear to wear a shoe on that foot. Emil felt ashamed and sorry for his stupid prank with the mousetrap. He wanted to make his father happy again and because he knew his father loved black pudding dumplings more than anything else he picked up the bowl of pudding mixture with both hands and held it out of the window.

'Look, Pappa!' he cried happily. 'We're having black pudding dumplings for dinner.'

His father lifted the straw hat from his face and stared miserably up at Emil. He hadn't forgotten the mousetrap incident yet, you could tell, which is why Emil tried extra hard to put it right again.

'Look at all this dumpling mixture!' he said cheerily and reached even further out with the bowl. But can you imagine what happened next? He lost his grip and the bowl and its blood-red mixture slipped out of his hands and right onto Emil's father as he lay there with his nose sticking up in the air.

'Blurp,' said Emil's father, because you can't actually say anything else when you've got dumpling mixture stuck all over your face. But he lifted himself slowly up from the grass and finally managed to let out a bellow, muffled by dumpling mixture at first, but after a while so loud it could be heard over the whole of Lönneberga. The earthenware bowl sat on his head like a Viking helmet and the red pudding mixture was running down his face and dripping all over him.

Just at that moment old Krösa-Maja came out of the brewhouse where she had been rinsing out the pig's intestines and when she caught sight of Emil's father covered in blood she screamed worse than the pig had done and tore off to the village with the terrible news.

'There bain't nort left of our precious farmer at Katthult!' she shouted. 'That Emil, that calamitous grommet, he's bashed him so's the blood's spurtin', heaven preserve us!'

But when Emil's mother saw what had happened she grabbed hold of his hand for a second time and rushed off with him at top speed to the tool shed. And while Emil, still in his nightshirt, sat there and carved his ninety-ninth little wooden man, Emil's mother had to work very hard to get his father clean.

'You could scrape off enough to make three or four dumplings, at least,' said Emil's father, but Emil's mother shook her head.

'What's gone is gone. We'll have to have potato pancakes instead.'

'Hee hee, we won't be having our dinner until tea time,' said little Ida, but then she went quiet because she caught sight of her father's eyes inside the dumpling mixture and they didn't look too happy.

Emil's mother put Lina to work grating potatoes for the pancakes. Perhaps you don't know what potato pancakes are? Well, they are a kind of pancake with grated potato in and they taste much nicer than they sound, I can promise you that. Soon Lina had made a lovely, thick, yellow mixture in the earthenware bowl which Emil's father had just taken off his head. He didn't want to go around looking like a Viking for the rest of the day. As soon as he was more or less cleaned up he went out into the fields to start cutting the rye while he waited for the pancakes to be ready.

That's when Emil's mother let Emil out of the tool shed.

Emil had been sitting still for a very long time and now he felt the need to move about.

'Let's play What a Wallop,' he said to little Ida, and Ida immediately raced off.

Now, What a Wallop was a running game Emil had made up. To play it you ran round as fast as lightning from the kitchen into the hall and from the hall into the bedroom and from the bedroom back into the kitchen and from the kitchen into the hall again, round and round as fast as your legs could go. The idea was to run in opposite directions, and off Emil and Ida went.

Every time they met they prodded each other in the stomach and yelled, 'What a Wallop!' That's how the game got its name and both Emil and Ida thought it was a hilarious game to play.

But when Emil, on his eighty-eighth lap, came charging into the kitchen he met Lina who was on her way to the stove, carrying the earthenware bowl in her hands, finally ready to make potato pancakes. And because Emil thought Lina ought to have a little fun too, he poked her in the stomach and shouted, 'What a Wallop!' He really shouldn't have done that. He knew how ticklish Lina was.

'Eeeek!' said Lina and in a flash bent over, just like a worm. And can you imagine what happened next? The earthenware bowl flew out of Lina's hands. Nobody really knows quite how it happened. The only thing they do know is that Emil's father, who had just come in through the door, absolutely starving hungry, got all the pancake mix slap in the middle of his face.

'Blurp,' said Emil's father again, because you can't actually say anything else when you've got pancake mix stuck all over your face. Emil and Ida made a little saying of it afterwards. 'Blurp said Pappa in the potato pancake mixture,' they used to say with a giggle, or 'Blurp said Pappa in the dumpling mixture.' It was just as funny whichever one you used.

But just at that moment Emil especially didn't have time to giggle because his mother grabbed hold of his hand and tore off with him at top speed to the tool shed. Behind him, Emil could hear his father bellowing, muffled at first by the pancake mixture but after a while so loud it could be heard over the whole of Lönneberga.

When Emil sat on the chopping block and carved his one hundredth little wooden man, he wasn't at all in the mood for a celebration. Quite the opposite! He was as angry as an irritated wasp! It was too much to have to sit in the tool shed three times in one day, he thought, and unfair, too.

'It's not my fault Pappa's in the way all over the place,' he burst out. 'You can't even set a mousetrap on the farm without him blundering into it. And why does he always have to put his ugly mug right where there's blood pudding mixture and potato pancake mixture flying about?'

Now, I really don't want you to think that Emil didn't like his father, or that Emil's father didn't like Emil. They liked each other very much, usually, but even people who like each other can fall out sometimes, when there's been a mishap with a mousetrap or blood pudding mixture or potato pancake mixture or something like that.

Saturday the twenty-eighth of July was coming to an end. Emil sat in the tool shed and got more and more angry. This wasn't how he had planned his one hundredth little wooden figure celebration. To start with it was Saturday night, so how could he invite Alfred to a party in the tool shed? Alfred had other things to do on Saturday nights. That's when he sat on the steps of his farmhand's cottage and got all cosy with Lina and played his accordion for her and certainly didn't have time to go to any party.

Emil threw down his penknife. He didn't even have Alfred. All alone, he was, and the more he thought about how people treated him, the more angry he became. What kind of behaviour was this, sitting around in only your nightshirt for a whole never-ending Saturday, not even having time to put on any clothes because of all this continual charging off to the tool shed? Well, if they wanted him in the tool shed, those Katthult Farm people, that's what they were going to get!

Emil banged his fist onto the workbench with a thump. Yes, *that's what they were going to get!* At that very moment Emil made a very serious decision. He was going to stay in the tool shed for the rest of his life. Wearing only his nightshirt and with his cap on his head, alone and abandoned by everyone, he would sit there for as long as he lived on this earth. Then they'll be happy and there won't have to be any unnecessary galloping backwards and forwards, either, he thought. Just don't try coming into my tool shed, that's all! If Pappa needs to saw a few planks, he won't be able to, and that's just as well because he'd only cut his thumbs off, that's for sure. Never known such a person for getting into trouble!

When the July evening was turning into twilight Emil's mother came and unbolted the door to the tool shed. The outside bolt, of course. She tugged at the door and realized it was still bolted on the inside. Then she smiled kindly.

'You don't have to be afraid any more, little

Emil. Pappa has gone to bed. You can come out now.'

But from inside the tool shed came a terrible 'Ha!'

'Why are you saying "Ha!"?' asked his mother. 'Open the door, dear, and come out!'

'I'm never coming out again,' said Emil in a low voice. 'And don't try coming in, otherwise I'll shoot!'

Emil's mother saw her little boy standing inside by the window with his rifle in his hand. At first she didn't want to believe that he was serious, but when she finally realized that he meant what he said she ran crying into the house and woke up Emil's father.

'Emil's sitting in the tool shed and doesn't want to come out,' she sobbed. 'What are we going to do?' Little Ida woke up, too, and immediately started howling and they all tore off to the tool shed, Emil's father, Emil's mother, and little Ida. And Alfred and Lina, who were sitting all lovey-dovey on the farmhand's doorstep, had to stop what they were doing, much to Lina's annoyance. Everyone had to help to get Emil out. At first Emil's father was very scornful.

'Oh, you'll come out when you get hungry,' he shouted.

'Ha,' said Emil again.

His father didn't know that Emil had a little tin stashed away behind the workbench, with a very useful supply of food, so there! He had cleverly made sure that he wouldn't die of hunger in the tool shed. He never knew from one day to the next when he would end up there and that's why he always had something to eat in his tin. At the moment there was bread and cheese and ham in there, as well as some dried fruit and quite a lot of biscuits. Soldiers have held out in their besieged forts with less food than that. Emil suddenly realized that the tool shed was exactly like a besieged fort and he was going to defend it against all his enemies. As stern as a military general he stood by the little window and took aim with his wooden gun.

'The first person to come close will get shot!' he shouted.

'Oh, Emil, sweetheart, don't talk like that! Come out!' sobbed Emil's mother. But that didn't help.

It didn't even help when Alfred said, 'Listen, Emil, if you come out we can go swimming in the lake, you and me!'

'Oh no,' yelled Emil bitterly. 'You just sit there on the step with Lina, why don't you? Me, I'll stay here!'

And that's what happened. Emil stayed put. And when nothing helped, not threats or pleading, they all eventually had to go in and go to bed, Emil's father, Emil's mother, and little Ida. It was a gloomy Saturday evening. Emil's mother and little Ida cried buckets and Emil's father sighed deeply as he climbed into his bed. He was used to his little boy sleeping over by the wall in his little bed, with his fluffy hair on the pillow and his gun and his cap beside him, and he missed him.

But Lina wasn't the sort to miss Emil and neither was she the sort who wanted to go inside to bed. She wanted to sit with Alfred on his doorstep and she wanted to sit there without being interrupted. That's why she was more than satisfied to have Emil in the tool shed.

'Though who knows how long the little menace will actually stay there?' she muttered to herself, and so she went ever so quietly and bolted the outside of the door again.

Alfred was playing his accordion and singing and didn't notice Lina's wicked deed. 'The cavalier he rides from the battlefield home,' sang Alfred. Emil heard it from where he sat on his chopping block, and he sighed deeply.

But Lina put her arms around Alfred's neck and nagged like she usually did and Alfred answered as he usually did:

'Well, I suppose I could marry you, if you really want me to, but there's no hurry.'

'Well, what about next year, then?' said Lina, not in the least put off, and then Alfred sighed louder than Emil and sang the song about a Lion and a Princess. Emil heard it, where he sat, and he started thinking what fun it would be to go to the lake with Alfred.

'Of course,' he said to himself, 'I could just go for a little swim with Alfred and then creep back into my tool shed again—if I felt like it.'

Emil rushed to the door and slid the bolt

back—but what good was that when that cunning Lina had bolted it from the outside? The door wouldn't open even though Emil threw all his weight against it. Then Emil understood. He knew immediately who it was who had locked him in.

'But I'll show her,' he said. 'She'll see all right.' He looked around the tool shed. It was getting quite dark in there. Once, when Emil had got up to something particularly mischievous, he had escaped through the window. But after that his father had nailed a plank across the outside of the window so that Emil wouldn't be able to do it again and fall into the nettle patch under the window. Emil's father really did care about his little boy and didn't want him to be covered in nettle stings.

'I can't get out through the window,' said Emil, 'and not through the door, either. And you won't catch me shouting for help. So how do I get out?'

He looked thoughtfully towards the fireplace. They had such a thing in the tool shed to keep it warm to work in the winter, and so that Emil's father could have a fire to heat up glue when he needed to.

'It's going to have to be up the chimney,' said Emil and he stepped up into the fireplace and right into the ash that had been left there since last winter and that now wrapped itself so gently around his bare feet and crept in between his toes. Emil peered up the chimney and then he saw something that made him laugh. It was the red July moon, peering down at him through the opening above.

'Hello, moon!' said Emil. 'Just watch me climb!' And leaning his back against the sooty wall of the chimney, up he went.

If you have ever tried to climb up a sooty chimney you will know how difficult it is and how dirty you get, but don't think Emil let that put him off.

Meanwhile poor unsuspecting Lina sat on the doorstep with her arms around Alfred's shoulders, with no idea what was going on. But Emil had said he would show her, and he did. Just as Lina decided to gaze up at the moon, she let out a scream which could be heard all over

Lönneberga.

'A myling!' cried Lina. 'There's a myling sitting on the chimney pot!'

Perhaps you've never heard of a myling before? Well, a myling was a small child ghost which people in Småland were very afraid of in the old days. Of course, Lina had heard Krösa-Maja's frightening stories all about small scary mylings which would suddenly appear, and that's why she shrieked wildly when she saw one sitting on the chimney pot, looking all black and terrifying.

Alfred also looked at the myling, but he only laughed.

'That little myling I recognize,' he said. 'Come down, Emil!'

Emil raised himself up in his sooty nightshirt and stood there on the roof as fierce as a warrior. He raised his sooty fist to the sky and shouted so that he could be heard over all of Lönneberga:

'This very evening the tool shed is coming down and I'll never ever sit in there again!'

Then Alfred went and stood by the shed wall, directly below Emil, and spread out his arms.

'Jump, Emil!' he shouted.

And Emil jumped, right into Alfred's arms. And then they both went down to the lake to have a swim. Emil needed that.

'I've never known a child like him,' said Lina, and she went indoors in a rage and lay down on her kitchen sofa.

But in Katthult Lake, among the white water lilies, Emil and Alfred swam up and down in the cool water, and in the sky the July moon hung like a red lamp, shining just for them.

'You and me, Alfred,' said Emil.

'Yep, you and me, Emil,' said Alfred. 'Just the two of us.'

The moon's reflection crossed the surface of the lake like a wide, shiny path but all around them the lakeside lay in deep darkness, because now it was night time and the end of the twenty-eighth of July.

But there were new days to come, and more mischief for Emil to get up to. Emil's mother wrote in the blue notebook until her arm ached and until the book was full of her scribbling, both backwards and forwards and up and down.

'I must get a new book,' said Emil's mother. 'It'll be Vimmerby market day soon, so I can buy a new one then, seeing as I'll be in town.'

•

And that's exactly what she did and it was lucky because how else would she have had room to write down all the mischief Emil got up to on market day?

'*May God give me strenth with that lad,*' she wrote. '*He'll go far if he lives long enuf to be grown wich his father does not beleeve will happen.*'

That's just where Emil's father was wrong and his mother right. Emil certainly did live long enough to grow up and actually went on to become leader of the local council and the most respected man in Lönneberga.

But for now we'll concentrate on what happened at Vimmerby market once when Emil was little.

WEDNESDAY THE THIRTY-FIRST OF OCTOBER:

Emil Finds Himself a Horse and Scares the Life Out of Mrs Petrell and the Whole of Vimmerby

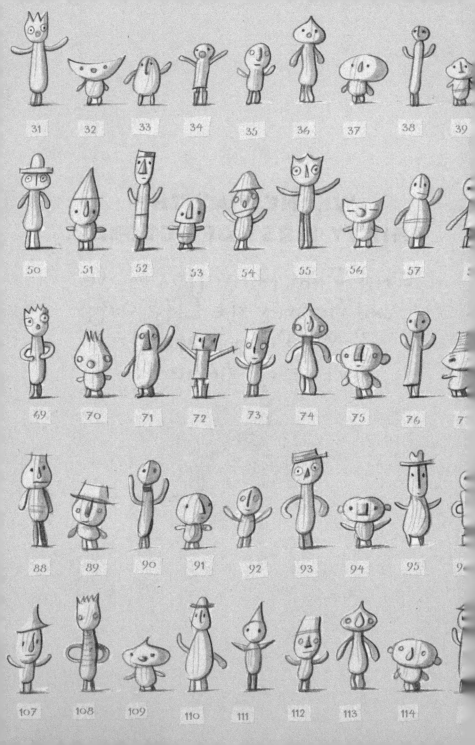

Every year on the last Wednesday in October there was a market in Vimmerby and there were goings on and high jinks in that town from early morning until late at night, I can tell you. Every single person from Lönneberga and the villages all around travelled there to sell cattle and buy oxen and trade horses and meet people and find themselves boyfriends and girlfriends and eat peppermint rock and dance the polka and get into fights and have fun, each in their own way.

Once, Emil's mother asked Lina whether she could list the special days of the year, because she wanted to find out exactly how bright Lina was, and Lina answered:

'Well, that would be Christmas and Easter

and Vimmerby market day, no less!'

So now you understand just why everyone was going to Vimmerby on the thirty-first of October, and already at five o'clock in the morning, in the pitch darkness, Alfred harnessed the two horses Markus and Jullan to the large wagon and off went the whole of Katthult: Emil's father and Emil's mother, Alfred and Lina, Emil and little Ida. Only Krösa-Maja was left at home to take care of the animals.

'Poor Krösa-Maja. Don't you want to come to the market, too?' asked Alfred, who was a kind soul.

'Do you think I'm mad?' said Krösa-Maja. 'Today? What, with that monstrous great comet coming? Not me. I wants to die here in Lönneberga where I belongs.'

You see, the people of Småland were going around waiting for a huge comet which was supposed to be on its way, and according to the *Vimmerby Times* it was on this very day, the thirty-first of October, that the comet would come hurtling through space and perhaps crash into the earth, smashing it into a thousand pieces.

You may not know what a comet is, exactly, and I hardly know either, but I think it's a piece of a star which has come loose and fallen off and is rushing around here and there in space. Everyone in Småland was scared to death of that comet which would destroy the entire world all of a sudden and put an end to all the fun.

'Of course, the wretched thing just *had* to arrive on Vimmerby market day,' said Lina angrily. 'Oh well, who cares? Perhaps he won't come until the evening, so us'll have time to get most things done anyhow!'

She smiled smugly and shoved her elbow into Alfred, who sat beside her on the back seat. Lina was expecting a lot from this day.

In the front seat sat Emil's mother with little Ida on her lap, and Emil's father with Emil on his lap. Guess who was driving the horses? It was Emil. I have forgotten to tell you how good Emil was with horses. It was Alfred who had taught him everything there was to know, from the very beginning, but in the end it was Emil who knew more about horses than anyone in the whole of Lönneberga, and could handle horses even better than Alfred could. So here he sat on his father's lap, driving like the best coachman ever—oh yes, that boy knew how to hold the reins, all right!

It had rained in the night, and mist and darkness lay like a veil over Lönneberga and the whole of Småland on this chilly October morning. It was still too early for any light to be showing over the treetops and the forest stood black and heavy with rain on each side of the track, as the people from Katthult came driving along in their wagon. But in spite of this, everyone was happy, and Markus and Jullan trotted along so briskly that the mud from the wet track flew up from their hooves.

Actually, Jullan wasn't quite as happy because she was old and didn't have much energy and what she wanted most of all was to stay at home in the stable. Emil had been nagging his father for a long time to buy a young horse to ride as a pair with Markus, and today would be a good day, thought Emil, seeing that they would be at the market.

But Emil's father said:

'You seem to think we're made of money! Oh no, old Jullan will have to keep going for another few years. Can't be helped.'

And Jullan certainly did keep going. She trotted bravely up the hills and Emil, who loved old Jullan, sang for her, as he always did when he wanted to cheer her up a bit:

> Me horse she canters pretty-oh.
> Wobbly knobbly-kneed she goes.
> That doesn't matter, though.
> She carries me, me gun, and hat,
> where roads are flat. I'm glad of that.

When at last everyone from Katthult Farm arrived at Vimmerby and found a safe place near the animal enclosure to leave Markus and Jullan, they all had different things they wanted to do. Emil's mother, with little Ida clinging on to her skirt, went to buy a blue notebook and to sell the wool and eggs that she had brought with her to the market. Lina wanted to go straight to the café with Alfred and drink coffee, and she managed to get him to go with her, even though he resisted and struggled at first, trying to break free so that he could go with Emil and Emil's father to look at the animal enclosure.

If you have ever been to Vimmerby on a market day then you will know what an animal enclosure is. You will know that it's where people buy and sell oxen and trade horses. Even at this early hour there was plenty going on in and around the enclosure. Emil just *had* to go there, that very minute, and his father was happy to go with him, even though he only planned to look and not to buy anything.

'Now don't forget we're invited to Mrs Petrell's for lunch at twelve o'clock,' was the last thing Emil's mother said before she disappeared with little Ida.

'You needn't worry I'd forget a thing like *that*,' said Emil's father, and off he went with Emil.

Well, Emil hadn't been at the animal enclosure more than five minutes before he caught sight of *the horse*!

The very horse he wanted and the one that made his heart go whoosh! What a horse! A beautiful little brown three year old, he was. He

stood tied to a fence and looked gently at Emil,
exactly as if he hoped Emil would want to buy
him. And Emil did want to buy him—oh, how he
wanted to! He looked around for his father so he
could start nagging him so ferociously that his

father would be *forced* to buy the horse to put an end to it. But do you know what had happened? His father had disappeared! He had decided to get himself lost in the crowd of farmers who were making such a noise with their shouting and laughing, and the horses that were neighing and stamping their feet, and the oxen and cows that were bellowing and mooing, all in one great big hullabaloo.

Isn't it always the way? thought Emil, crossly. You can't take him anywhere. The first thing he does is disappear.

And time was running out. Already a very self-important horse dealer from Målilla was swaggering up, his eyes fixed on Emil's horse.

'How much does that one cost?' he asked the farmer who was looking after the horse. A pale skinny thing he was, from the town of Tuna.

'Three hundred kronor,' said the Tuna farmer, and when he heard that, Emil's heart sank. Trying to get three hundred kronor out of his father would be like trying to get blood out of a stone, he knew that. But I'll try anyway, Emil thought, because he was the most stubborn child in the whole of Lönneberga, and the whole of Småland, come to that. So he set off quickly through the crowds of people to try and find his father. He rushed here and there, getting crosser and crosser, grabbing hold of all sorts of farmers who he thought were his father because they looked like him from behind. But when he spun them round, it turned out to be a complete stranger from Södra Vi or Locknevi, and never Anton Svensson from Lönneberga.

But don't think a little thing like that made Emil give up hope! There was a flagpole in the animal enclosure and quick as a flash Emil climbed up to the top and shouted as loudly as he could:

'Is there anyone here who recognizes this little lad? His father's got lost!'

Then he noticed something happening down there among the hurly-burly of farmers and cows and horses below him. A kind of pathway opened up through the uproar and someone came tearing towards the flagpole at top speed, and it was none other than his father.

Anton Svensson shook his little boy down

from the flagpole as if he were a ripe apple tumbling down from an apple tree, and then he grabbed hold of his ear.

'You wrrrretched child!' he said. 'Where did you get to? Do you have to run off the minute you get here?'

Emil had no time to answer.

'Come with me!' he said. 'You've got to see this horse.'

And sure enough Emil's father did see the horse—but it was already sold! Wasn't that awful? Emil and his father turned up just in time to see the horse dealer from Målilla pull out his wallet and take out three one hundred kronor notes which he slapped into the Tuna farmer's hand.

And Emil cried.

'You're sure this horse is well-behaved?' asked the horse dealer.

'Oh yes, he's no trouble,' answered the Tuna farmer. But he looked away when he said that, as if he was thinking of something else.

'I notice he hasn't been shod yet,' said the horse dealer. 'I'll have to see to that, before I go home.'

Emil stood there, crying, and his father felt sorry for his little boy.

'Don't cry, Emil,' he said, and then he nodded decisively. 'We'll go and buy a bag of peppermints for you, and hang the expense.'

And he took Emil to the square where the ladies who sold sweets sat at their sweet stalls, and he spent ten öre on striped peppermints for Emil.

But then he bumped into another farmer from Lönneberga and started chatting to him and forgot all about Emil. Emil stood there with his mouth full of peppermints and his eyes full of tears and thought about the horse. Suddenly he caught sight of Alfred, with Lina hanging on to him. He looked very tired, poor Alfred, and that was no wonder, because Lina had dragged him backwards and forwards past the jeweller's shop seventeen times, and each time she had tried to get him to go inside so that he could buy her an engagement ring.

'And if I hadn't dug in my heels as hard as I could, no one knows how it would have ended,' said Alfred, delightedly. He was more than happy to see Emil, of course. Emil quickly told him all about the horse and they stood there sighing because the horse would never be coming to Katthult. But then Alfred bought Emil one of those clay whistles that looks like a bird—and sounds like a bird when you blow into it too—from the potter who stood in the square selling his goods.

'You can have that as a market day present from me,' said Alfred, and that made Emil feel immediately happier inside, in the place where before all the sadness had been.

'Oh, so it's all right to buy whistles what go tweet tweet,' said Lina. 'Anyhows, when's that there comet going to turn up? I think about now would be a good time.'

But there was no sign of any comet and it wasn't quite twelve o'clock, so it didn't have to hurry itself for a while.

Alfred and Lina had to go and see if Markus and Jullan were all right and to eat their lunch. They had a picnic hamper in the wagon. Emil would rather have gone with them but he knew he had to have lunch at Mrs Petrell's house at midday, so he looked around for his father. And believe it or not his father had disappeared *again*! He had taken the chance to get lost among all the market people and sweet ladies and potters and basket weavers and brush makers and barrel organ players and other market goings-on.

'Never known anyone like him for getting lost,' said Emil. 'Next time I come to town he's staying at home, because I'm not putting up with this any more.'

But Emil didn't give up just because his father had run off. He had been to town before and knew more or less where Mrs Petrell lived. She had a small, neat, white-painted house with a conservatory at the front, somewhere along the main street. It wouldn't be impossible to find, thought Emil.

Mrs Petrell was one of the finest ladies in Vimmerby so it was a little odd that she had invited the family from Katthult Farm to lunch. I wonder if it had something to do with the fact that Emil's mother usually brought along some of her tasty sausages—she couldn't be that sausage-mad, surely? Perhaps not, but it was true that Mrs Petrell always seemed to be coming to parties at Katthult. Parties at cherry-time, cheesecake parties, and all sorts of other festivities where there were sausages and spare ribs and roast veal and meatballs and omelettes and jellied eels and things like that. And you can't keep going to parties without inviting people in return, thought Mrs Petrell. 'You've got to be fair,' she said, and that's why she had chosen this market day, when the Katthult family would be in town anyway, and had invited them to come at midday. She planned to treat them to warmed-up leftover fish pie and blueberry soup.

Mrs Petrell had eaten at eleven o'clock, just a little roast beef and a large slice of marzipan gateau, because there wasn't much fish pie to go round. And that would certainly look good, wouldn't it, if she tucked into the pie herself and her guests didn't have enough to fill themselves up—no, she couldn't possibly do that!

They were there already, seated around the table in the conservatory: Emil's father, Emil's mother, and little Ida.

'That wrrrretched child! It would be easier to

hang on to a fist full of eels. They don't wriggle away nearly as fast as he does,' said Emil's father.

He meant Emil, of course.

Emil's mother wanted to rush off straight away and look for her little boy, even though Emil's father had assured her he had looked everywhere.

But Mrs Petrell said, 'If I know Emil, he'll be able to find his way here perfectly well.'

Mrs Petrell never spoke a truer word. At that very minute Emil was on his way through her front door, but then he just happened to catch sight of something that stopped him in his tracks.

Next door to Mrs Petrell lived the town's mayor in a beautiful house surrounded by gardens, and in among the apple trees was a boy wobbling around on stilts. It was the mayor's little Gottfrid. He caught sight of Emil and immediately fell on his head in a lilac bush. If you have ever tried to walk on stilts then you will understand why. It isn't so easy to balance on a pair of those long poles with only a little wedge to rest your foot on. But Gottfrid soon stuck his nose out of the bush and looked at Emil with interest. When two small lads who are as alike as two peas in a pod meet for the first time, a gleam comes into their eyes. Gottfrid and Emil looked at each other and smiled silently.

'I'd really like a hat like you've got there,' said Gottfrid. 'Can I borrow it?'

'Nope,' said Emil, 'but you can let me borrow your stilts.'

Gottfrid thought that was a good bargain.

'Though I don't think you'll be able to walk on them,' he said. 'It's too difficult.'

'We'll see,' said Emil.

He was braver than Gottfrid had thought. In an instant he was up on the stilts and wobbling quickly off between the apple trees. Lunch with Mrs Petrell had been completely forgotten. Meanwhile, in her conservatory, the Katthult family had finished off the fish pie. That was quickly done and then it was time for the blueberry soup. There was more than enough of that in a huge tureen which stood in the middle of the table.

'Eat up,' said Mrs Petrell. 'I hope you're hungry.'

She wasn't very hungry herself and didn't touch the blueberry soup, but she made up for it by talking. It was the huge comet she talked about, because that's what everyone in Vimmerby was talking about that day.

'It would be frightful,' she said, 'if a comet were to put an end to everything.'

'Yes, who knows. This blueberry soup might be the last thing we eat in this lifetime,' said Emil's mother, and then Emil's father quickly stretched out his bowl.

'Perhaps I could ask for a little more,' he said, 'just to be on the safe side.'

But before Mrs Petrell had time to serve him, something terrible happened. There was a crash and a shriek, something came flying through the big pane of glass behind Mrs Petrell and suddenly there was glass and blueberry soup all over the conservatory.

'The comet!' screamed Mrs Petrell, and dropped to the floor in a faint.

But it wasn't a comet. It was only Emil, who came crashing through the window like a cannonball and fell with his head right in the blueberry soup so that it flew all over the place.

Oh dear, what a commotion there was in the conservatory! Emil's mother shrieked and his father bellowed and little Ida cried. Mrs Petrell was the only one who stayed calm but that, of course, was because she had fainted flat out on the floor.

'Quick, out to the kitchen and get some cold

water!' yelled Emil's father. 'We've got to cool her down!'

Emil's mother rushed off as fast as she could and Emil's father rushed off after her, to make it go faster.

Emil slowly crawled out of the soup tureen, his whole face bright blue.

'Why do you always have to be in such a hurry when you eat?' lectured little Ida. Emil ignored her.

'Gottfrid is right,' he said. 'You can't get over the fence on stilts. I've proved *that* at least.'

But then he noticed Mrs Petrell lying on the floor and felt very sorry for her. 'Why does it have to take this long to fetch a little water,' he said. 'We're in a hurry here, you know!'

Emil knew exactly what to do next. He swiftly picked up the tureen with the blueberry soup and emptied everything that was left right onto Mrs Petrell's face. And believe me or not, it helped!

'Blurp,' said Mrs Petrell and was up on her feet in a flash. And now you know what a good idea it is to make *lots* of blueberry soup, in case of accidents.

'I've already cured her,' said Emil proudly, when his mother and father finally came running out of the kitchen with the water. But his father glared at him darkly and said:

'I know someone who's going to be cured in the tool shed when we get home.'

Mrs Petrell was still feeling dizzy and her face was all blue, too, just like Emil's. But Emil's mother, who always knew what to do, and was very good in emergencies, laid her down on the sofa and grabbed hold of a scrubbing brush.

'We'd best get this cleaned up,' she said, and set to with the brush, first on Mrs Petrell and then on Emil and then on the conservatory floor. Soon there wasn't a trace of blueberry soup to be seen, except for the tiniest drop inside one of Emil's ears. His mother swept up all the pieces of broken glass, too, and his father dashed off to the glaziers for a new pane of glass which he then put back in the window where the old one had been. Emil went and stood by him and was keen to help but his father wouldn't let him get anywhere near the pane of glass.

'Keep away,' he said through gritted teeth. 'Clear off and don't come back until it's time to go home!' Emil had nothing against clearing off. He was happy to go and have another chat with Gottfrid. But he was hungry. He hadn't had a bite to eat apart from a tiny slurp of blueberry soup which he thought he might as well eat seeing that he was in the soup tureen at the time.

'Any food in your house?' he asked Gottfrid, who was still standing on his side of the fence in the mayor's garden.

'Loads and loads,' said Gottfrid. 'It's my pappa's fiftieth birthday today and we're having a party. There's so much food the larder door won't close.'

'Good,' said Emil. 'I could taste it, if you like, to check it's not too salty.'

Gottfrid didn't take long to make up his mind. He went into the mayor's kitchen and came back out with lots and lots of wonderful food piled on a plate: cocktail sausages and meatballs and pies and all sorts of things. Then they stood there, Gottfrid and Emil, one on each side of the fence, and ate everything. Emil was full up and happy.

Until Gottfrid said:

'We're having a firework display tonight. The biggest there's ever been in Vimmerby!'

Emil had never seen a firework display in his entire life. They didn't have time for such nonsense at Katthult. And now he was bitterly disappointed that there was going to be a huge firework display and he wasn't going to be able to see this one *either* because everyone from Katthult Farm had to get off home long before evening came.

Emil sighed. This was turning out to be a miserable market day, all right. No horse, no fireworks, just a lot of trouble and the tool shed waiting for him when he got home. That was what it had all come to.

Dismally he said goodbye to Gottfrid and went to find Alfred, his friend who cheered him up when he was feeling sad.

But where was Alfred, exactly? The streets were jammed full of local people, farmers, and visitors, all mixed up together, and trying to find Alfred in that confusion was not going to be easy. Emil trotted around looking for him for several hours and during that time got into quite a lot of trouble, things that never did get written up in a blue notebook, because nobody ever found out. But Alfred was nowhere to be found.

It gets dark early in October in Småland. Soon it would be dusk. Soon this market day would be over for ever. The farmers at the market were already beginning to think about getting along home and the people of Vimmerby should also have been thinking about going indoors, you would have thought, but they didn't want to. They wanted to carry on laughing and chatting and being boisterous on the streets, and they all looked strangely excited—well, just think what a day this was! Market day and the mayor's birthday and perhaps the last day on earth, if that comet really was going to come hurtling by. You can understand, I'm sure, that it felt a little strange for the people of Vimmerby to be walking about there in the twilight, waiting, not knowing whether it was something thrilling or something terrible they were waiting for. When people are afraid and happy at the same time they make more noise than usual, which is why there was such a lot of hoo-ha and hullabaloo out on the streets, but the houses stood quiet and still and nobody was at home apart from the cat and one or two old grannies who had to look after the grandchildren.

If you have ever strolled around in a small town like Vimmerby, perhaps on just such a market day as this one, and perhaps at twilight, then you'll know what fun it is to walk along the cobblestoned streets, peeping in through the windows of the little houses at grannies and grandchildren and the cat, and how exciting it is to creep off along dark alleys and through gateways and find yourself in murky backyards where the visiting farmers have lined up their carts and wagons and are standing around having a beer before harnessing the horses and setting off, each to his own home. Emil thought it was good fun and exciting, too. Soon he had forgotten that he had been feeling sad and he was sure he would find Alfred sooner or later. And he did—but not before he found something else.

Just as he was walking along a narrow back street he heard a loud commotion coming from a dark stable yard. There were men swearing and shouting and a horse was whinnying. Emil dived straight in through the doorway to find out what was going on. And there he saw something that stopped him in his tracks. There in the stable yard was an old smithy and in the glow from the blacksmith's fire he saw his horse, his little brown horse, in the middle of a scrum of men who were all furiously angry. And guess why they were angry? Because the little brown horse would not let them shoe him. As soon as the blacksmith tried to lift the horse's leg he would begin to buck and kick and shove the men around in all directions. The blacksmith scratched his head and didn't know what to do.

'I've shod many horses in my time,' he said, 'but I've never seen anything like this.'

Do you know what a blacksmith is? It's someone who puts shoes on horses, because horses need shoes just as much as you do, you see, otherwise they would wear out their hooves and fall and hurt themselves when the roads were slippery. They don't wear ordinary shoes, of course, but a kind of curved strip of iron which is nailed onto their hooves— horseshoes, in fact. Perhaps you have seen one.

Well, the little brown horse had clearly decided he wasn't going to have any shoes. He stood as still and angelic as anything, just as long as no one touched his back legs, but as soon as the blacksmith got anywhere near his back legs there was the same circus as before and the horse kicked himself free, even though there were half a dozen men trying to hold him. The horse dealer from Målilla, the man who had bought the horse, was getting more and more annoyed.

'Let me do it myself,' he said at last and angrily grabbed one of the horse's back legs. But he was given such a kick that he was sent flying right into the middle of a puddle.

'Well, I could have told you that would happen,' said an old farmer who was standing watching. 'You can't shoe that horse. Believe me, they've tried back home in Tuna twenty times at least.'

That's when the horse dealer realized he had been tricked into buying the horse, and that made him even angrier.

'Take the lump of horsemeat, anyone who wants him!' he yelled. 'I can't stand the sight of him!'

And who should step forward but Emil. 'I'll take him,' he said.

But the horse dealer only laughed. 'You, you little whippersnapper!'

He hadn't really meant what he said about giving away the horse but because so many people had heard him say it, he would now have to try and find some clever kind of way to get out of the situation, which is why he said:

'Well, of course you can have the horse, if you can hold him still while we shoe him!'

They laughed at that, all the people standing around, because they had all tried themselves and they knew that this was a horse no one could control. Now, I don't want you to think Emil was a stupid boy. Oh no, he knew more about horses than anyone else in the whole of Lönneberga and the whole of Småland, come to that, and when the little brown horse kicked and bucked and whinnied as hard as he could, Emil thought:

He's behaving just like Lina does at home, when you tickle her!

That was precisely the problem and Emil was the only one to realize. The small horse was ticklish, that's all. That was why he kicked and snorted and shoved, just like Lina, and when he neighed so wildly it was only because, just like Lina, he was killing himself laughing as soon as anyone came near his back legs—well, you know yourself what it feels like to be tickled.

So Emil went up to the horse and took hold of his head between his own strong little hands.

'Now listen here,' he said. 'You're going to be shod, so don't make a fuss because I promise I won't tickle you.'

Guess what Emil did next? He walked around the horse until he stood behind him, and then very quickly he took hold of one of the back hooves and lifted it up. And the horse simply turned his head and looked mildly at Emil, as if he wanted to see what Emil was doing.

Because, you know, a horse has no more feeling in its hooves than you have in your nails, so you can understand that just there he was not the slightest bit ticklish.

'Here you are,' said Emil to the blacksmith. 'Come on, where's the shoe? I'm holding.'

Then a kind of murmuring went round the crowd who were watching, and the murmuring continued while Emil helped the blacksmith shoe all four of the horse's hooves.

But when it was finished the horse dealer tried to wriggle out of the agreement. He remembered what he had promised and he didn't want to keep his promise. Instead, he took a five kronor note out of his wallet and held it out to Emil.

'This ought to be enough, I'm sure,' he said.

But then the farmers, the ones who had been watching, got angry, because they themselves were fair and always kept their word.

'Don't try it on,' they said. 'Give the boy the horse!'

And that's what happened. The horse dealer was rich, everyone knew that, and so to keep up appearances, he did as he had promised.

'Oh well, three hundred kronor isn't the end of the world,' he said. 'Take the stupid animal and get out!'

Can you imagine how happy Emil was then! He jumped up on his newly-shod horse and rode out through the gates like a fine general. All the farmers cheered and the blacksmith said:

'This is the kind of thing as happens, when it's Vimmerby market!'

Straight through the bustle of the market rode Emil, beaming with pride and happiness, and on the main street, in the middle of the most crowded part of all, who was walking along but Alfred.

He stopped suddenly and stared, his eyes wide open.

'Jumping Jehosephat,' he said. 'Where did that horse come from?'

'He's mine,' said Emil. 'He's called Lukas and you know what? He's just as ticklish as Lina.'

At that very moment Lina came rushing up and grabbed Alfred's sleeve.

'We'm on our way home,' she said. 'Farmer's hitching the horses.'

So, that was the end of all the fun. Everyone from Katthult Farm had to go back to Lönneberga again. But there was one thing Emil had to do first—he had to show Gottfrid his horse.

'Tell Pappa I'll be there in five minutes,' he said, and he rode off to the mayor's house, clattering over the cobblestones.

The October twilight had fallen over the mayor's house and garden but all the windows shone festively and from inside came the sound of laughter and chatter. The mayor's party was well under way.

Walking around in the garden was Gottfrid. He didn't like parties. He had gone back to his stilts instead. But he went crashing on his head into the lilac bush as soon as he saw Emil come riding up.

'Whose horse is that?' he asked, when he had managed to get his nose out of the bush.

'Mine,' said Emil. 'He's *mine*!'

Gottfrid didn't believe that at first, but when he finally realized it was true, he flew into a rage.

Hadn't he nagged his father every day from morning to night to buy him a horse? And what had his father said every time?

'You're too young. There aren't any boys of your age who have their own horse!'

What a whopping great lie! Because here was Emil, his father could see that for himself, if he had eyes in his head and would only come out and have a look! But his father was indoors, sitting at the table and having a party, Gottfrid explained to Emil. He was stuck in there with a load of idiots who only drank and talked and made never-ending speeches.

'I'll never be able to get him to come out,' said Gottfrid miserably, and tears welled up in his eyes.

Emil felt sorry for Gottfrid but he was never stuck for ideas. If the mayor wouldn't come to the horse, then the horse would have to come to the mayor, it was as simple as that. All he had to do was ride up the steps and go through the front door, straight through the hallway and into the dining room. All Gottfrid had to do was open the doors.

If you have ever been at a party where a horse has suddenly come in, then you'll know that some of the people there gaze in amazement and give a kind of jump, exactly as if they have never seen a horse before. They did that at the mayor's party, too. Especially the mayor. He jumped and got a piece of cake stuck in his throat which is why he couldn't utter a sound in reply when Gottfrid shouted:

'Well, what have you got to say now, then?

Some people *do* have horses!'

Everyone else at the party was overjoyed that a horse had turned up, as they would be, of course, because horses are such nice animals. They all wanted to pat Lukas. Emil sat on his horse and smiled contentedly. He was perfectly happy to let them pat his horse. But then an old major came up and wanted to show how good he was with horses. He tried to squeeze Lukas's back leg, but oh dear, oh dear, he had no idea how ticklish Lukas was!

The mayor had managed to get the piece of cake out of his throat and was just about to tell Gottfrid a thing or two when, at that very moment, the major pinched Lukas's back leg. The next second a pair of hooves flew out and thumped a little side table which was standing there, and suddenly an entire birthday cake covered in cream came flying across the room and landed with a splosh right in the middle of the mayor's face.

'Blurp,' said the mayor.

Strangely enough, everyone roared with laughter when that happened, but they didn't know any better. The mayor's wife was the only one who didn't laugh. She didn't dare. She came running up, anxiously waving a cake knife. All that mattered now was to get scraping immediately so that her poor husband could have a pair of peepholes to look through, at the very least. Otherwise he wouldn't be able to see what was happening at his own birthday party.

Suddenly Emil remembered that he should have been going home to Lönneberga and so he rode very quickly out through the door. Gottfrid came running after him—he couldn't talk to his father anyway because he was covered in whipped cream, and also Gottfrid couldn't bear to tear himself away from Lukas.

Out by the gate, Emil was waiting to say goodbye to him.

'You're so lucky,' said Gottfrid, patting Lukas for a last time.

'Yes, I know,' answered Emil. Gottfrid sighed.

'But at least we're going to have fireworks,' he said, as if to make up for it. 'So that's all right!'

He showed Emil all the different fireworks laid out ready on the garden table by the lilac bushes, and something clicked in Emil's head. He knew he was in a hurry, of course, but you see he had never seen a firework display in his life, poor thing.

'I could try lighting one for you,' he said. 'Just to see if they work all right.'

It didn't take Gottfrid long to make up his mind.

He picked one of the fireworks out of the pile.

'Well, only this tiny firecracker, then,' he said. Emil nodded and climbed down from the horse.

'All right, only this tiny firecracker. Can you give me a match?'

He got one. And pop, pop, pop, the sparkling little firecracker leapt away—oh, yes, it was working all right. It jumped backwards and forwards and finally ended up back on the garden table, in the middle of all the other fireworks. I expect it didn't want to be alone. But Gottfrid and Emil didn't notice because all of a sudden someone shouted behind them. It was the mayor, striding down the front steps, wanting to have a word with them. By now he had managed to get most of the cream off his face, except for his moustache, which shone in the October darkness.

All the while the people of Vimmerby were strolling around the streets, laughing and cheering and shouting, not knowing whether to expect something exciting or something terrible.

And then it came! The dreadful thing that they had all been waiting for, secretly shuddering inside, happened!

All of a sudden the sky began to glow over by the mayor's house and then the heavens were full of fizzing snakes and shining balls and rushing trails of fire, and they exploded and popped and banged and crackled in such an awful way that the poor Vimmerby people turned pale with fright.

'The comet!' they shrieked. 'Help! We're going to die!'

And there was a shouting and a wailing that had never before been heard in that town, because everyone thought their last hour had come. Those poor people! No wonder they shrieked and passed out in heaps on the streets. Only Mrs Petrell sat completely calm in her conservatory as she watched the balls of fire whizz around outside.

'I don't believe in comets any more,' she told the cat. 'I bet you anything you like that Emil has been up to his tricks again.'

Mrs Petrell never spoke a truer word. It certainly was Emil and his little firecracker that had made all the birthday fireworks go off with a bang and shoot into the air all at once.

But how lucky it was that the mayor happened to come out just at the right moment, otherwise he wouldn't have seen anything at all of his firework display. Now he was standing right in the middle of all the whizzing and exploding and had his work cut out trying to leap out of the way every time a ball of fire came whistling past his ears. Emil and Gottfrid were sure he was enjoying himself because he kept giving delighted little yelps every time he leapt out of the way. It was only when a rocket happened to shoot up one of his trouser legs that he seemed to get angry, otherwise why else would he have let out such an enormous bellow and carried on yelling his head off non-stop while he charged off to the water butt round the corner of the house and like a madman plunge his leg into it?

But that's not what you should do with rockets, because then they go out, you see. He should have been able to work that one out for himself.

'Well, at last I've seen a firework display,' said Emil, as he lay hidden behind the mayor's woodshed with Gottfrid beside him.

'Yes, now you really have seen a firework display,' said Gottfrid.

Then they kept quiet and waited. Not for anything in particular, just until the mayor stopped buzzing around the garden like a big angry bee.

But when the Katthult Farm wagon set off for Lönneberga a short while later, all the coloured sparkles and balls of fire had long since gone out. Only the stars shone above the tops of the pine trees. The forest was dark, and so was the road, but Emil was happy.

And he sang in the darkness as he went riding along on his horse.

Hey hop, Pappa, look!
What a horse I've got!
What legs, what a trot,
What a gallop he's got!

And his father sat up on the driving board and steered the horses, more than satisfied with his Emil. All right, the lad might have frightened Mrs Petrell and the people of Vimmerby half to death with his pranks and this comet business, but hadn't he also managed to get hold of a horse absolutely free? That put everything else in the shade. No one else in the whole of Lönneberga had such a boy and there would be no tool shed this time, oh no, thought Emil's father.

In fact, he was in a recklessly good mood, perhaps because just before he was about to set off for home he had met an old friend who bought him several bottles of excellent Vimmerby beer. Not that he usually drank beer, you understand—not Emil's father, oh no, he wasn't that sort—but if someone was offering and it was absolutely free, what else was he to do?

Emil's father cracked the whip merrily as he drove along, and said proudly:

'Here comes Farmer Anton from Katthult, such an *important* man!'

'Well, well,' said Emil's mother. 'What a good job it isn't market day every day. How lovely it will be to get home!'

Little Ida slept on her lap with her present from the market held tightly in her hand. It was a small china basket filled with china roses. Written on it was 'Greetings from Vimmerby'.

And in the back seat Lina slept, leaning against Alfred's arm. Alfred's arm was asleep, too, because Lina had been resting on it for such a long time, but apart from that he was wide awake and in a tremendously good mood, just like Emil's father, and he said to Emil who rode along beside him:

'Tomorrow we'll be muck spreading all day. That'll be fun.'

'Tomorrow I'll be riding my horse,' said Emil. 'All day. That'll be fun.'

And just at that moment the wagon lurched around the very last bend in the track and there ahead of them they could see the light shining in the kitchen window at Katthult, where Krösa-Maja had their dinner waiting.

Now, you might be thinking that Emil would stop getting up to mischief, now that he had a horse, but that wasn't the case. For two whole days he rode Lukas, but by the third day, that would be the third of November, he was ready to get going again. Guess what he did? Hoho! It makes me hoot with laughter when I think about it! You see, it just so happened that on that day . . . no, stop! *Stop!* I promised Emil's mother that I would never tell anyone what he did on the third of November, because it was actually after that little episode that the people of Vimmerby collected that money, you remember, wanting to send Emil to America. Emil's mother would rather not think about it afterwards— she didn't even write it up in her blue notebook, so why should I tell you about it? No. But instead you can hear what Emil got up to on Boxing Day that year.

MONDAY THE TWENTY-SIXTH OF DECEMBER:

When Emil had the Great Obliteration Party at Katthult and Trapped the Sergeant-Major in the Wolf Pit

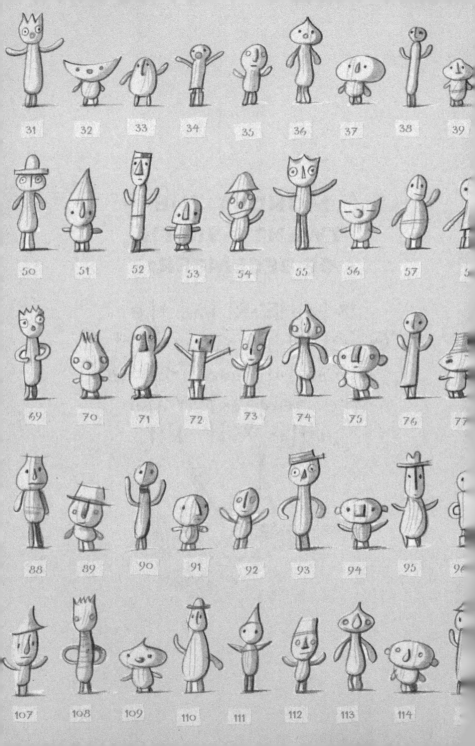

31   32   33   34   35   36   37   38   39

50   51   52   53   54   55   56   57   5

69   70   71   72   73   74   75   76   77

88   89   90   91   92   93   94   95   96

107   108   109   110   111   112   113   114

Before it can be Christmas you have to get through the chilly, rainy, dark autumn, and that isn't much fun wherever you live. It wasn't much fun in Katthult, either. Alfred trudged along behind the oxen in the drizzle, ploughing the small stony fields, and following on after him in the furrows trotted Emil. He helped Alfred shout at the oxen that were unbearably slow and stubborn and couldn't understand the point of ploughing. But at least it got dark early, and that's when Alfred unharnessed the oxen and they could lumber off home, the oxen, Alfred, and Emil. Alfred and Emil stepped over the kitchen doorstep with great lumps of mud on their boots, which drove Lina mad because she had just scrubbed the kitchen floor.

'She's such a fusspot,' said Alfred. 'Whoever marries her won't get a minute's peace as long as he lives.'

'That'll be you, then,' said Emil.

Alfred went quiet and thought for a while.

'Know what? I don't think it will,' he said at last. 'I don't dare. But I don't dare tell her, neither.'

'Do you want *me* to?' asked Emil, who was ever so brave and fearless. But Alfred didn't want him to.

'It has to be said nicely,' he said. 'So as not to upset her.'

Alfred went around for a long time trying to work out the nicest way to tell Lina that he didn't want to marry her, but he couldn't come up with a good way to do it.

The heavy darkness of autumn lay over Katthult Farm. The oil lamps in the kitchen had to be lit as early as three o'clock in the afternoon, and after that everyone sat there together and got on with various things. Emil's mother had a spinning wheel and spun delicate white wool which she would use to make socks for Emil and Ida. Lina carded the wool with her two prickly wooden paddles, getting it ready for spinning, and so did Krösa-Maja, when she was there. Emil's father mended shoes and by doing that saved lots of money which otherwise would have gone to the village shoemaker. Alfred was just as thrifty, he darned his own socks. They always had big holes in the toes and heels, but Alfred

quickly stitched them up. Lina was really keen to help him, but Alfred wouldn't let her.

'Oh no, because then I'm done for,' he explained to Emil. 'Then it won't matter how nicely I say it.'

Emil and Ida usually sat under the table, playing with the cat. Once Emil tried to convince her that the cat was actually a wolf, and when she didn't want to believe that, he made such a loud wolf howl it made everyone in the kitchen jump. His mother wanted to know why he had done it, so Emil said:

'It's because there's a wolf under the table.'

Well, that set off Krösa-Maja, who immediately started to tell them all about wolves, and Emil and Ida crept closer to her, happy to listen. They were about to hear something terrible, they knew that, because it was only terrible things Krösa-Maja talked about. If it wasn't murderers and thieves and ghouls and ghosts, then it was about people having their heads chopped off and horrendous fires and dreadful accidents and deadly diseases and dangerous animals. Such as wolves, for example.

'When I were a girl,' Krösa-Maja began, 'there was many wolves in Småland.'

'But then King Karl the Twelfth came along and shot them all, which was just as well,' said Lina.

That made Krösa-Maja very angry because even though she was old, she was not as old as Lina thought.

'You talk as if you knows all about it,' said Krösa-Maja and then she wouldn't tell them any more. But Emil got round her and at last she set off again, telling them lots of horrendous tales about wolves and how people used to dig wolf pits to trap them, when she was a girl.

'So King Karl the Twelfth, he wasn't needed any more,' began Lina, and then stopped herself hastily. But it was too late. Krösa-Maja was angry again, and that wasn't surprising. Karl the Twelfth was a king who had lived hundreds of years before, you see, and Krösa-Maja certainly wasn't that ancient.

But Emil got round her again, and so she told them all about werewolves, which were the worst of the wolves and crept about only when the moon was full. Werewolves could talk, said Krösa-Maja, because they weren't ordinary wolves but something in between a wolf and a human being and they were the most dangerous monsters of all. If you happened to meet a werewolf in the moonlight then your number was up, because the werewolf was the worst beast of all. That's why people ought to stay indoors at night time, when the moon is full, said KrösaMaja, and glared at Lina.

'Although Karl the Twelfth . . . ' began Lina.

At that Krösa-Maja threw down her carding paddles and said she had to be getting off home because she felt so old and tired.

That evening, when Emil and Ida lay in their beds in the bedroom next to the kitchen, they started talking about werewolves again.

'What a good thing there aren't any nowadays,' said Ida.

'Aren't there?' said Emil. 'How do you know, when you haven't got a wolf pit to trap any in?'

He lay awake for a long time thinking about trapping wolves and the more he thought the more certain he became that if you had a wolf pit then you probably would be able to get a wolf to fall in it. And because he liked to get things done, the very next morning he set about digging a wolf pit in the gap between the tool shed and the outside food store. That was the place where lots of nettles grew in the summer time, but now that it was winter they lay black and wilted on the ground. It takes quite a long time to dig a wolf pit. It has to be deep enough so that the wolf won't be able to climb out once it has fallen in. Alfred helped Emil with the digging from time to time, but despite that it was almost Christmas before the wolf pit was finished.

'Not that it matters, neither,' said Alfred. 'Those wolves, they don't come out of the forest till it be winter time and freezing and they be starving hungry.'

Little Ida shuddered when she thought of all the starving wolves out there in the forest that would come padding about on cold winter nights and start howling under the windows. But Emil didn't shudder. He looked at Alfred with shining eyes and enjoyed thinking about the wolf that would fall into his pit.

'All I've got to do now is cover it over with branches and sticks so the wolf doesn't see where the hole is,' he said happily, and Alfred agreed.

'You'm right! You've got to be wily, as Batty-Jack said when he couldn't find his fishing line and tied the worm on to his toe.'

That's a saying they used to have in Lönneberga, but Alfred shouldn't have said it because actually Batty-Jack was his grandfather who lived in the poorhouse, the place where the old people of Lönneberga went to when they had no money and nowhere to live, and you shouldn't make jokes about your own grandfather. Alfred didn't mean any harm, he really didn't. He was only saying what everyone else said.

Well, all they had to do was wait until the very coldest part of winter arrived, and arrive it did. A few days before Christmas a cold snap set in and it began to snow and snow and snow. It snowed over all of Katthult and over Lönneberga and Småland, too, until everything looked like one big snowdrift. All you could see were the tops of the fences that surrounded the farm. You could just about work out where the farm tracks were, and there was not a living soul who could see that somewhere between the tool shed and the food store there was a wolf pit. Over the pit the snow lay soft and white like a carpet and Emil prayed to God every night that his sticks and branches wouldn't break under the weight of the snow before a wolf came tumbling in.

This was the time when everyone at Katthult was in a rush, because Christmas was celebrated properly on the farm, believe me. First there was the big Christmas wash. Lina and Krösa-Maja lay on the ice-covered jetty by the Katthult stream and rinsed the laundry. It made Lina's fingernails split and she cried and blew on her aching fingers. Then the huge Christmas pig was slaughtered and there was hardly any room left in the kitchen, said Lina, because of all the black pudding dumplings, boiled sausages and fried sausages and smoked sausages, which were all crammed together with hams and spare ribs and goodness knows what else.

There was juniper beer, too, because it was Christmas. Emil's mother brewed it in the big wooden trough out in the brewhouse. And there was enough bread-making going on to make you dizzy: sandwich loaves and sourdough bread and fine rye bread and saffron bread and cinnamon buns and ginger biscuits and crunchy twists and meringues and little doughnuts and small fairy cakes and—well, you couldn't count them all. And then there were the candles, they had to be made, too. Emil's mother and Lina worked late into the night dipping candles, big ones and little ones, and tiny ones for the tree, because here at Katthult they celebrated Christmas in a big way, I can tell you that!

Alfred and Emil harnessed Lukas to the log sledge and drove out into the forest to look for a Christmas tree, and Emil's father went down to the barn and hunted for the couple of sheaves of corn that he had put aside for the sparrows.

'This is madness right enough,' he said, 'but I suppose the sparrows have got to survive, them too, at Christmas time.'

But there were more to think about, too, who had to survive at Christmas time: all the destitute old people in the poorhouse.

I don't expect you know what destitute means,

or what a poorhouse is, come to that, and be glad you don't. The poorhouse was something they had in the old days and if I were to tell you what it was really like, well, that would be far worse than all Krösa-Maja's stories about murderers and ghosts and wild animals. If you can imagine a small, run-down cottage with a couple of rooms full of poor, worn-out old people who have nowhere else to go and who live there all together in one big muddle of dirt and lice and hunger and misery, well, then you know what it is to be destitute and live in the poorhouse.

The one they had in Lönneberga was probably no worse than any other poorhouse, but it was still a terrible place to end your days when you got old and couldn't look after yourself any longer.

'Poor Grandfather,' Alfred used to say. ''Tisn't much of a life. But it would be better if that Sergeant Major weren't such an old battleaxe.'

The Sergeant Major was the old woman who was in charge at the poorhouse. I mean, she was one of the poor people, too, but she was the biggest and the strongest and the most bad-tempered and that's why she had been put in charge of the poorhouse, which would never have happened if Emil had by this time been a grown-up and leader of the local council. But for now he was still a little boy and could do nothing about the Sergeant Major. Alfred's grandfather was afraid of her and so were the other poor people who lived there.

'Lo, she goes forth like the roaring lion among the sheep,' Batty-Jack used to say. He was a bit odd, was Batty-Jack, and spoke as if he was reading out of the Bible, but he was kind and Alfred was very fond of his grandfather.

The old people who lived in the poorhouse hardly ever got enough to eat, which was a dreadful state of affairs, thought Emil's mother.

'Poor old folks! They ought to have something nice at Christmas time, they too,' she said. And that's why a couple of days before Christmas Emil and Ida came trudging through the snow up the hill to the poorhouse carrying a large basket between them. In the basket Emil's mother had packed all sorts of delicious food. There were sausages of every kind, there was ham and bacon, there were loaves of bread and black pudding dumplings, saffron buns and ginger biscuits, there were candles and a little pouch of tobacco for Batty-Jack.

Anyone who has had to go hungry for a long, long time will understand how overjoyed everyone in the poorhouse was when Ida and Emil stepped through the door with their basket. They wanted to start eating straight away, old Batty-Jack and Karl the Spade, Johan One Kronor and Crazy Niklas, Mia-Fia and Little Iris Tubs, Big Hat Bettan and Holy Amalia and all the others. But the Sergeant Major said:

'Not before Christmas Eve, let's get that straight right away!'

And nobody dared argue with her.

Emil and Ida went home and soon it was Christmas Eve. They had so much fun at Katthult that day, and on Christmas Day, too. That was when they set off for the early morning service at the church in Lönneberga, and Emil beamed with pride as he travelled in the big sleigh, because Lukas and Markus cantered so fast that the snow whirled around their hooves and they left all the other sleighs behind. All through the church service Emil sat very still and as quiet as a mouse. Yes, he behaved himself so well that his mother wrote in her blue notebook:

'That Boy reely is a good littel soul and does not get up too mischiff in Cherch leastways.'

Emil continued being well-behaved through-out the whole of the long Christmas Day. He and Ida played so nicely with their Christmas presents and a wonderful feeling of peace lay over Katthult.

But then came Boxing Day and Emil's mother and father were invited to a party over in Skorphult some miles away. Everyone in Skorphult knew about Emil and so children weren't invited.

'Well, I don't care,' said Emil. 'It's worse for the people of Skorphult, poor things. At this rate they'll never get to meet me!'

'Nor me, neither,' said Ida.

Lina was meant to stay at home and look after the children that day, but she had been whining since early morning because she wanted to go and visit her dear old mother who lived in a cottage near Skorphult. She thought she could go with Emil's mother and father in the sleigh, because they were going in that direction.

'Oh, I can look after the children,' said Alfred. 'There's plenty of food and I can make sure the young 'uns don't play with matches and suchlike.'

'Yes, but you know what Emil's like,' said Emil's father, looking despairingly into space. But then Emil's mother said:

'Emil is a sweet little boy and he won't get into any trouble, leastwise not when it's Christmas. Stop snivelling, Lina, you *can* come with us.'

So that's what happened.

Alfred and Emil and Ida stood by the kitchen window and watched the sleigh disappear over the slopes and when it was completely out of sight Emil leapt happily into the air like a little goat.

'Whoopee! Now we'll have some fun!' he said, but then Ida pointed her tiny finger towards the track.

'Look, here comes Batty-Jack,' she said.

'Well, so it is,' said Alfred. 'What's up, I wonder?' You see, Batty-Jack wasn't allowed to go out. He was a bit funny in the head and couldn't manage on his own. Well, that's what the Sergeant Major said, anyway.

'He's always wandering off,' she said. 'I haven't got time to run around looking for him when he goes and gets himself lost.'

But Batty-Jack could find his way to Katthult without any trouble and here he was, walking up the track looking like a little crumpled brown paper bag, with his white hair flapping around his ears. Soon he was standing sniffing in the kitchen doorway.

'We ain't had none of them black pudding dumplings,' he said. 'No sausages, neither. The Sergeant Major has took everything.'

Then he couldn't say any more, because he was crying so much.

That's when Emil got angry. He shook with rage so much that Alfred and Ida could hardly bear to look at him. A wild look came into his eyes and he grabbed a china bowl from the table.

'Just let me get at that Sergeant Major!' he shouted, and hurled the bowl at the wall so that it smashed into pieces and scattered all over the kitchen. 'Where's me gun!'

Alfred felt really afraid.

'Take it easy,' he said. 'It's dangerous to get so angry.'

Then Alfred hugged and comforted his poor old grandfather and wanted to know why the Sergeant Major had done such a terrible thing, but the only thing Batty-Jack could say was:

'We ain't had none of them black pudding

dumplings. No sausages, neither. And I ain't had me to-to-tobacco,' he sobbed.

Then Ida pointed in the direction of the track again.

'Look, here comes Iris Tubs,' she said.

'She's come to takes me 'ome,' said Jack, and he began to tremble all over.

Iris Tubs was a little busybody and the Sergeant Major used to send her to Katthult as soon as Jack went missing. That's where he usually went because Alfred was there, of course, and Emil's mother, who was so kind to the poor.

It was Iris Tubs who told them everything that had happened. The Sergeant Major had hidden the food in a cupboard up in the attic, where it was cold and a good place to store food this time of year. But when she came to get the basket on Christmas Eve, one tiny, wrinkled little sausage was missing, and the Sergeant Major flew into a terrible rage.

'Like a roaring lion among flocks of sheep,' said Batty-Jack, and Iris Tubs agreed with him. Goodness me, what an enormous fuss the Sergeant Major had made about that sausage, and she would not rest until she had found out who the guilty person was who had stolen it.

'Otherwise it will be a Christmas here what will make God's angels weep,' she had said. And it was, Iris Tubs assured them of that. You see, nobody would admit to taking the sausage, however loudly the Sergeant Major shrieked and carried on. Some of the old people thought the Sergeant Major had made it all up just so she could keep all the tasty food for herself, but whatever had happened it certainly did turn out to be a Christmas to make God's angels weep, so Iris Tubs said. The Sergeant Major had stayed in her room up in the attic all Christmas Eve. She lit the candles and ate sausages and black pudding dumplings and ham and saffron buns until she almost exploded, the fat old baggage, but down in the poorhouse below the others sat around and cried and had only a little salt herring to eat, even though it was Christmas.

And it was the same on Christmas Day. The Sergeant Major told them right at the beginning that no one would have as much as half a black pudding dumpling until the thief came forward and confessed, and while she was waiting for that to happen she sat up in her own room and ate and ate and spoke to no one. Iris Tubs herself had peeped through the keyhole at her every hour and had watched as all the lovely food that Emil's mother had sent was shovelled down the Sergeant Major's throat. But now she was afraid that Batty-Jack had gone to Katthult to tell on her, which was why she had told Iris Tubs that it was a matter of life or death that he was brought home this very minute.

'So you see, 'tis best we go now, Jack,' said Iris Tubs.

'Dear old Grandad,' said Alfred. 'It's a shame being poor.'

Emil said nothing. He sat on the log box and ground his teeth. He sat there for a long time after Batty-Jack and Iris Tubs had disappeared and you could see he was thinking. But finally he thumped the log box with his fist and said:

'I know someone who's going to have a party!'

'Who's that?' asked Ida.

Emil thumped the log box once again.

'Me,' he said, and he told them what he had

planned. There was going to be *an enormous party* like never before and every single person in Lönneberga poorhouse was going to come to Katthult, right at that very moment!

'Yes, but Emil,' said little Ida anxiously, 'are you sure this isn't one of your pranks?'

Alfred was worried, too, and thought it might well be a prank, but Emil assured him that it wasn't one at all. It was a good deed which would make all God's angels clap their hands just as much as they had cried over the miserable Christmas in the poorhouse.

'And Mamma will be happy, too,' said Emil.

'Yes, but what about Pappa?' said Ida.

'Hmm,' said Emil. 'Well, anyway, it isn't a prank.' Then he went quiet and thought again.

'But getting them out of the lion's den, that'll be the tricky part,' he said. 'Come on, let's go there and try!'

By this time the Sergeant Major had stuffed her face with every single sausage and dumpling, all the ham, every saffron bun and ginger biscuit, and made sure she had used up every bit of Batty-Jack's tobacco as well. Now she was sitting in her attic room, feeling sorry for herself, which you do feel when you have done something very wrong and eaten far too many dumplings, too. She didn't want to go down to the others, either, because they just glared at her and sighed and wouldn't say a word.

But just as the Sergeant Major was sitting there feeling rather unhappy, she heard someone bang on the front door, so she hurried down the stairs to see who had come.

It was Emil who stood there on the steps. Emil from Katthult. That made the Sergeant Major worried. What if Emil had come because Batty-Jack or Iris Tubs had been there telling tales about her!

But little Emil bowed politely and said:

'I was wondering if I left my penknife behind when I was here last time?'

He was artful, that Emil! The penknife lay safe and secure in his own trouser pocket all the time, but he needed an excuse for coming to the poorhouse, and that's why he said it.

The Sergeant Major assured him she hadn't seen any knife. And that's when Emil said:

'Were the sausages good? And the dumplings, and everything?'

The Sergeant Major lowered her eyes and stared down at her broad feet.

'Yes, yes, they were,' she said quickly. 'Oh yes, your dear mother at Katthult, she knows just what us poor folks need. Do thank her so *very* much.'

And that's when Emil said what he had come all the way to the poorhouse to say, but he said it very casually:

'Mother and Father have gone to a party in Skorphult,' he said.

Suddenly the Sergeant Major seemed very keen.

'A party at Skorphult? I never knew about that.'

No, otherwise you would have been there a long time ago, thought Emil. He knew just like everyone else in Lönneberga, that if there was a party somewhere, the Sergeant Major would soon turn up at the kitchen door, as sure as eggs were eggs. And you couldn't get rid of her until she had tasted some cheesecake, at least. She would go through fire and water to have cheesecake, and if you have ever been to a party in Lönneberga then you know as well as the Sergeant Major that on the table there will be long rows of cheesecakes in shiny copper dishes, which the guests have brought as a present.

'Seventeen cheesecakes,' said Emil. 'What do you think of that?'

Of course Emil couldn't possibly know whether they had seventeen cheesecakes at Skorphult, and he didn't say he did, either, because he didn't want to lie. No, he just said, very cleverly:

'Seventeen cheesecakes, what do you think of that?'

'Well, I never did,' said the Sergeant Major. Then Emil left. He had done what he came to do.

He knew that in half an hour the Sergeant Major would be on her way to Skorphult.

And Emil was absolutely right. He and Alfred and little Ida watched from behind a pile of logs and saw the Sergeant Major come out, wrapped in her thickest woollen shawl and with her begging bowl under her arm. She was on her way to Skorphult. But can you imagine—the old dragon *locked* the door from the outside! Well, that was a fine thing to do! Now those poor old people were locked in just as if they were in a prison, and the Sergeant Major thought it was just as well they were. Just let BattyJack try escaping again! He'd soon see who was in charge around here!

And with that the Sergeant Major trotted off towards Skorphult as fast as her fat legs could carry her.

Emil went up to the door and pulled at it, to see how good the lock was. Alfred tried, too, and little Ida, but it was locked all right, no doubt about it.

By this time all the old people had gathered in the window and were looking out, frightened by the three figures outside who wanted to come in. But Emil yelled:

'You'll be coming to a party at Katthult, if we can only get you out of there!'

Then a hum of voices could be heard from inside the poorhouse, like bees in a hive. This was an amazing, unheard-of event but a hopeless one at the same time, for they were locked in and how in the world were they going to get out?

Now you might be wondering why they

didn't simply open a window and climb out—
would that have been so difficult? Well, clearly
you have never heard of inside windows. During
the winter you couldn't open a window in the
poorhouse because of the inside windows. They
were panes of glass, nailed over the windows
that were already there, but on the inside, with
the gaps all around them stuffed with strips of
paper to stop the wind whistling through. But
then how could you let in any fresh air, you may
be thinking? You dear child, don't ask such a daft
question! Who has said that fresh air was allowed
into the poorhouse? They weren't interested in
such silly ideas because there was plenty of fresh
air coming down the chimney and through the
cracks in the walls and floor, thank you very
much, and no one wanted any more.

No, getting out through the window was out
of the question for these poor old souls. There
was *one* window that could be opened, but that
was in the Sergeant Major's room up in the attic
and there was not one single little old person
from the poorhouse who would make a leap of
four metres just to go to a party, however hungry

they were, because that would mean leaping right into the kingdom of heaven, that's for sure.

But Emil didn't let a small thing like that put him off. He searched around and found the ladder which had been stored under the woodshed and he put it up against the Sergeant Major's window, which Iris Tubs had been more than happy to open for him. Up the ladder climbed Alfred. He was big and strong and he had no trouble carrying the poorhouse people, who were tiny and thin. Of course they oohed and aahed but out they came, all of them. All apart from Holy Amalia. She didn't dare and neither did she want to. But Big Hat Bettan promised to bring back as much party food as she could carry, which made Amalia happy.

If someone had been travelling on the Katthult road on this particular Boxing Day just as it started to get dark, he would have thought it was a row of grey ghosts he saw before him who came hobbling, struggling, and puffing up the hills to Katthult. And they did look like ghosts, it's true, in their rags, those poor old people, but they were as happy as larks and as eager as children—oh my, oh my, it had been such a long time since they had been to a Christmas party! It also made them gleeful to think that the Sergeant Major would soon be coming home to find the poorhouse empty apart from one little old woman.

'Hee hee, serves her right,' said Johan One Kronor. 'Hee hee, there she'll be, with none of us there. See how she feels then!'

At that they all laughed in delight. But when they finally came into the kitchen at Katthult, which was all beautifully decorated for Christmas, and Emil had lit the five large candlesticks so that the candlelight was reflected in the newly polished brass pans hanging on the walls, making everything shine and glow, they feil silent. Batty-Jack thought he had gone up to heaven.

'Lo, there is light and holiness everlasting,' he said, and cried, because crying was something Batty-Jack did when he was happy and when he was sad.

That's whenEmil said:

'*Let the party begin!*'

And the party did begin. Emil and Alfred and little Ida helped each other to carry out as much as they could manage from the larder. And now I think you should know everything that was put on the kitchen table in Katthult that Boxing Day, when they had finished carrying it all in.

On the table was:

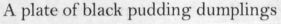

A plate of black pudding dumplings
A plate of pork sausages
A plate of liver paté
A plate of smoked sausage
A plate of meatballs
A plate of veal cutlets
A plate of spare ribs
A plate of boiled sausages
A plate of fried sausages
A plate of herring salad
A plate of salt beef
A plate of salted ox tongue
A plate of extra fine sausages
A plate with the big Christmas ham
A plate with the big Christmas cheese
A plate with a big loaf of bread
A plate of sourdough bread
A plate of rye bread
A tankard of juniper ale

A jug of milk
A saucepan of rice pudding
A dish of cheesecake
A bowl of prunes
A dish of apple pudding
A bowl of whipped cream
A bowl of strawberry jam
A bowl of pears in ginger and
A little roast suckling pig decorated
with icing squiggles.

That was all, I think. I can't have forgotten more than three or four things—well let's say five at the most, to be on the safe side, but otherwise I've remembered everything.

And they sat around the table and waited very patiently, all the poorhouse inmates, and tears filled their eyes with every dish that was brought in.

Finally Emil said:

'Help yourselves! Tuck in!'

And so they tucked in, they really did, in a flash! Alfred and Emil and little Ida ate too, but Ida couldn't swallow more than a couple of meatballs because she had started thinking. She had started wondering whether this wasn't perhaps a prank after all. She had suddenly remembered that tomorrow, the day after Boxing Day, oops, that's when all the relations from Ingatorp were supposed to be coming to Katthult! And here was all the party food disappearing in all directions! She listened to the crunching and the munching and the slurping and the smacking of lips around the table. It was as if a herd of ravenous wild animals had thrown themselves over the bowls and dishes and plates. Little Ida understood that only desperately hungry people eat like that, but it was still a terrible thing to hear. She tugged at Emil's arm and whispered so that no one else could hear:

'Are you *sure* this isn't a prank? Remember they are coming from Ingatorp tomorrow!'

'They are fat enough as it is,' said Emil calmly. 'Surely it's better the food goes where it's needed most.'

But even so, he began to get a bit worried himself because it looked as if there wasn't going to be more than half a dumpling left over. What wasn't gobbled up was slipped into pockets and bags, and the plates were emptied in a flash.

'Now I've obliterated the herring salad,' said Mia-Fia. Obliterated—what Mia-Fia meant was that she had eaten it all up and the plate was empty.

'Now us has obliterated everything,' said Batty-Jack at last, and never had he said a truer word. That is why to this very day the party has been known as 'The Great Obliteration Party at Katthult' and it was talked about for ages afterwards in Lönneberga and the villages around, I can tell you that.

There was only one thing left and that was the little roast suckling pig. He stood there on the table, gazing sadly with his icing sugar eyes.

'Mercy me, that pig looks like a little ghost,' said Mia-Fia. 'I wouldn't want to get started on him!'

She had never seen a whole roast piglet before and neither had any of the others. That's why they felt a kind of respect for the little pig and didn't touch him.

'Be there possibly by any chance any sausages left?' asked Karl the Spade when all the plates had been emptied. But Emil said that at this point there was only one small sausage left in the whole of Katthult and that was sitting on a stick outside in his wolf trap. There it would sit and lure any passing wolf, so Karl the Spade couldn't have it, and neither could anyone else.

Then Big Hat Bettan let out a yelp.

'Holy Amalia!' she shrieked. 'Us has forgotten all about her!'

She looked around in confusion, not knowing what to do, and her eyes fastened on the piglet.

'She may as well have that thing, our Amalia, even if it does look like a ghost. What do you think, Emil?'

'Well, I suppose she can have the pig, then,' said Emil with a sigh.

Now they were all so full that they could hardly move and it was completely impossible for them to drag themselves back to the poorhouse on their own old legs.

'We'll have to take the log sledge,' said Emil. They had a log sledge at Katthult, a hulking great thing they called Old Lumber. On Old Lumber there was room for as many poorhouse inmates as you wanted, even if they were at the moment a little fatter than usual.

By now it was evening and the stars burned brightly in the sky. There was a full moon, newly fallen snow, and no wind, a glorious night for a sledge ride. Alfred and Emil helped them all onto Old Lumber. At the front sat Big Hat Bettan with the suckling pig, then all the others one by one, with little Ida, Emil, and Alfred right at the back.

'Away we go!' shouted Emil.

And away they went, down the hills at Katthult with the snow flying in clouds around them and all the old people shouting for joy. Oh, how they shouted! It was a long time since they had been for a sledge ride. Only the pig sat quietly at the front, held safely in Big Hat Bettan's hands, staring ghostlike into the darkness.

And what about the Sergeant Major—where had she been all this time? Well, I'll tell you. I wish you could have seen her when she came home from her cheesecake outing to Skorphult! Seen her walking home in her grey woollen shawl, fat and full-up, taking out the key and putting it in the lock, chuckling to think how meek and docile they would be by now, all the old codgers in there. Oh yes, they had to learn who was in charge, and that was the Sergeant Major and no mistake!

So now she turns the key, now she goes over the doorstep, now she's in the hall . . . but why is it so quiet? Are they asleep already, the old dears, or sitting there sulking silently? The moon shines in through the poorhouse window, lighting up every corner—why is there not a single living soul to be seen? *Because there isn't anyone there!* Oh no, Sergeant Major, there is not a living soul there!

That's when the Sergeant Major starts shaking all over. She is more afraid than she has been in her entire life. What kind of person can walk through locked doors? None other than God's angels . . . yes, that was it! The poor creatures who she has tricked out of their sausages and dumplings and tobacco, they have been taken by God's angels to a much better place than the poorhouse. She is the only one to have been left behind, wailing in misery. Oh, oh, oh! The Sergeant Major howls like a dog. But then a voice is heard from one of the beds over by the wall, where a figure lies pitifully huddled under a blanket.

'What are you making such a fuss about?'

says Holy Amalia.

Guess how quickly the Sergeant Major springs into life again! How quickly she manages to force everything out of Amalia! She's like that, is the Sergeant Major. And then she sets off running as fast as she can to Katthult. It's about time they came home, her old people. It has to be done fast and it has to be quietly, so there won't be too much gossip about it in Lönneberga.

Katthult is looking so beautiful there in the moonlight. The Sergeant Major sees how all the candles have lit up the kitchen windows. And now she feels ashamed all of a sudden and can't bring herself to go in. She would like to be able to peep through a window first and find out if it really is her poor old inmates who are sitting in there, having a party. But she would need a crate or something else to stand on, otherwise she won't reach to see in. The Sergeant Major takes a little walk down to the tool shed to see if she can find something. And she does find something, but it's not a crate. She finds a sausage. How amazing! There's a lovely little sausage sitting on the end of a stick right there in the middle of the snow, in the moonlight! Now, the Sergeant Major is so full of cheesecake she could burst, but she knows how quickly you can get hungry again, and to let a whole sausage sit there and go to waste would be madness, thinks the Sergeant Major. So she takes a step. One great, long step.

That was how they trapped wolves in Småland in the old days.

At that very moment, just as the Sergeant Major was plummeting into the wolf pit, the party at Katthult finished and all the old people were climbing onto the sledge for the journey home. But not a sound came from the wolf pit, because the Sergeant Major didn't want to call for help straight away. She thought she would be able to drag herself out on her own, and that's why she kept silent.

Her poorhouse inmates sped down the slopes in a cloud of snow and arrived back at the poorhouse to find the door open, strangely enough. They staggered in and went straight to bed completely beside themselves with food and sledging, but happier than they had been for many years.

And Emil and Alfred and little Ida turned back towards Katthult in the light from the moon and the stars. Emil and Alfred pulled the sledge up the hills but Ida was allowed to sit on it because she was so little.

If you have ever been out with your sledge on the slopes around Lönneberga on such a still, moonlit night, you will know how strangely quiet everything is, almost as if the whole world lay fast asleep. If you have, you may well be able to imagine how terrifying it is, right in the middle of all that silence, to hear an eerie howling. Here came an unsuspecting Emil and Alfred and Ida, up the last hill, when they suddenly heard from over by Emil's wolf pit a howling enough to make your blood run cold. Little Ida turned pale and just at that moment longed for her mother. But not Emil! He took a leap of pure joy in the snow.

'A wolf's landed in me wolf pit!' he shouted. 'Oh, where's me gun?'

The howling got louder and louder the closer they got to Katthult, so you would have thought the whole forest was full of wolves that were howling in answer to the cries of the wolf that was trapped.

But then Alfred said, 'That's a very strange sound for a wolf! Listen!'

And they stood still in the moonlight and listened to the wolf's terrible wailing.

'Help, help, *help*!' it cried. Then Emil's eyes lit up.

'A werewolf!' he shouted. 'I do believe it's a werewolf!'

In a couple of leaps he reached the wolf pit before the others. And that's when he saw what kind of wolf it was he had trapped. Not a werewolf at all but that detestable old Sergeant Major! Emil was furious—what business did she have being in his wolf pit! He wanted a *real* wolf. But then he stopped to think. Perhaps the Sergeant Major had fallen into his trap for a purpose. The idea struck him that he could teach her a lesson, so that she would be a bit kinder and not so bad-tempered—yes, it occurred to him that perhaps she could actually be taught how to behave properly! Because she certainly needed to do that. And that's why he shouted to

Alfred and Ida:

'Oh-ho! Come over here! Come and have a look at this ugly old beast!'

And they stood there all three, staring down at the Sergeant Major who, in her grey shawl, did look something like a wolf.

'Are you sure that's a werewolf?' said little Ida, her voice shaking.

'It certainly is,' said Emil. 'A bad-tempered old lady werewolf is what it is, and they are the most dangerous of all.'

'Yep, for them's so greedy,' said Alfred.

'And look at that one,' said Emil. 'She's probably gobbled a lot in her time. But that's all over now. Alfred, hand over me gun!'

'Oh, no, dear little Emil, can't you see who it is?' shrieked the Sergeant Major, because she was scared to death when Emil started talking about his gun. She didn't know it was only a toy gun which Alfred had carved for Emil.

'Did *you* hear what the werewolf said, Alfred?' asked Emil. 'Because I didn't catch it.'

Alfred shook his head. 'Nope, I didn't hear either.'

'And I don't care, anyway,' said Emil. 'Where's me gun, Alfred?'

Then the Sergeant Major shouted, 'Can't you see it's *me*? I'm stuck here, aren't I?'

'What's she saying?' Emil asked Alfred. 'Did she say she was stuck down there with her auntie? Just as long as she's not down there with her uncle, too, otherwise the trap will be full to bursting with old werewolves. Me gun, Alfred!'

That's when the Sergeant Major began to wail at the top of her voice.

'You're too cruel and that's for sure,' she sobbed. 'Can I help it if I was just dumped in here?'

'Dumpling? Did she say she liked dumplings?' wondered Emil.

'I think she did,' said Alfred. 'But we haven't got any dumplings.'

'Nope, there's no more dumplings left in the whole of Småland,' said Emil. 'Because that Sergeant Major has stuffed herself full of them.'

Then the Sergeant Major started wailing even worse than before because now, of course, she realized that Emil knew how badly she had treated Batty-Jack and the other poor old people. She howled so much that Emil felt sorry for her, because he had a good heart, that boy. But if changes were going to be made in the poorhouse, the Sergeant Major could not be let off too lightly, which is why Emil said:

'Do you know what, Alfred? If you look really closely at this werewolf, it almost looks a bit like that Sergeant Major over in the poorhouse.'

'Oh, holy mackerel!' said Alfred. 'The Sergeant

Major is worse than all the werewolves in the whole of Småland!'

'Know what I think?' said Emil. 'I reckons werewolves are sweet little things compared to the Sergeant Major. For she doesn't like anyone else to have anything. By the way, I wonder who it was who pinched that sausage out of the cupboard?'

'It was me!' whined the Sergeant Major. 'It was *me*! I'll admit anything if you'll just get me out of here!'

Then Alfred and Emil looked at each other and smiled quietly.

'Alfred,' said Emil, 'haven't you got eyes in your head? Can't you see that it *is* the Sergeant Major! It's not a werewolf!'

'Jumping Jehosephat!' said Alfred. 'How could we have been so mistaken?'

'Don't ask me,' said Emil. 'They are alike, it's true, but a werewolf hasn't got a shawl like that, I'm sure.'

'Nope, it hasn't! But werewolves have got whiskers too, haven't they?'

'Shame on you, Alfred! Now you be nice to

the Sergeant Major,' said Emil. 'Go and fetch a ladder!'

So a ladder was lowered down to the Sergeant Major in the pit and she climbed up it, howling loudly all the time. Then she ran away leaving a trail of whirling snow behind her, because she was off from Katthult for ever. She never wanted to set foot in the place again. But before she disappeared over the brow of the hill, she turned and shouted:

'Yes, it was me who took the sausage, may God forgive me, but I had forgotten that on Christmas Eve. I swear I had forgotten.'

'Then it was a good job she had to sit here for a while and remember,' said Emil. 'Wolf pits aren't such a stupid idea after all.'

The Sergeant Major stumbled down the hills as fast as her fat legs could carry her, and she was quite out of breath when she got back home to the poorhouse. They were fast asleep by now, all her poor old people, in their flea-ridden beds, and the Sergeant Major didn't for the life of her want to wake them up. That's why she crept in as silently as a ghost— never had she moved so quietly.

They were all there, safe and sound, all her oldies, and she counted them like sheep. Batty-Jack and Karl the Spade, Johan One Kronor and Crazy Niklas, Mia-Fia and Iris Tubs—they were all there, she could see. But suddenly she saw something else. On the table beside Holy Amalia's bed stood . . . Oh, saints preserve us, there stood a ghost, yes, it certainly was a ghost, even though it looked like a pig, an awful little moonlit pig! Or perhaps nothing less than a werewolf that stood there staring at her with its frightening white eyes!

So many frightful things in one day—it was too much for the Sergeant Major. With a sigh she sank down onto the floor. There she lay and did not wake up again until the sun shone in through the poorhouse window and it was the day after Boxing Day.

The day after Boxing Day—that was the day the relations from Ingatorp were supposed to be coming to Katthult for a party. Oh dear, oh dear, oh dear—what kind of party was that going to be? Oh well, it would sort itself out. There was freshly salted pork out in the food store, and fried pork with potatoes and onion gravy was food good enough for a king, should the occasion arise.

But Emil's mother was very sad when she wrote in her blue notebook that evening, I have to admit, and to this day the page has stains just as if someone's tears had dropped onto it.

'Writing on the day after Boxing Day, in the evening, with grate sadness,' was the heading she wrote. And below: *'Today he has sat in the tool shed the hole day, the poor child. Of corse he is reely good that lad only sumtimes I think as how he has lost his senses.'*

But life in Katthult went on. Soon the winter was over and the spring came. Emil sat often in the tool shed, and when he wasn't doing that he played with Ida and rode on Lukas and drove along with the milk churns and teased Lina and chatted with Alfred, and as time went on got into more mischief which made his life interesting and varied from morning to evening, so that by the beginning of May he had no less than one hundred and twenty-five little carved men on the shelf in the tool shed—what a clever boy!

Alfred didn't get up to mischief but he had problems anyway. You see, he hadn't yet dared mention to Lina about that thing, you know, about not wanting to marry her.

'It's probably best that *I* do it after all,' said Emil, but Alfred wouldn't hear of it.

'It has to be said nicely, I've told you that, so she doesn't get sad.'

Alfred really was a kind soul but he didn't have the slightest idea how he could say that thing to Lina nicely. But one Saturday evening at the beginning of May, when Lina was sitting on the doorstep of the farmhand's cottage, stubbornly waiting for him to come out and get all lovey-dovey with her, that's when Alfred decided that *now* was the time to do it! So he leaned out of the cottage window and shouted to her:

'Know what, Lina? There's something I've been wanting to tell you for ages!'

Lina giggled a little. It looked as if now she was going to hear something she so very much wanted to hear.

'What is it, Alfred dear?' she called back to him. 'What is it you want to say?'

'Well, that marrying-type thing we've talked about . . . you know what? I think we'll stuff the idea!' Yes, that's what he said, poor Alfred! It's awful to have to tell you such a thing, because I don't want to teach you any bad expressions, at least not more than you know already. But you must remember that Alfred was only a poor farmhand in Lönneberga, and you're not. He couldn't come up with a nicer way to say it,

even though he had puzzled over it so long, poor Alfred!

Lina wasn't sad, though.

'That's what you think,' she said. 'But you'll soon see!'

And at that very moment Alfred understood that he would never get away from Lina. But for this evening at least he wanted to be happy and free, which is why he went with Emil down to Katthult Lake and settled down to do some pike fishing. It was such a beautiful evening, the kind you can almost only get in Småland. All the wild cherry trees around the lake were in bloom, the blackbirds were singing, the mosquitoes hummed, and the pike were biting. They sat there, Emil and Alfred, and watched their floats bobbing about in the water. They didn't say much but they were happy enough. They sat there until the sun began to set, and then they went home, Alfred with the pike on a stick and Emil blowing a little wooden flute that Alfred had made for him. Through the meadow they went, along a winding trail under the birch trees with their bright green spring leaves. Emil blew his flute and amazed the blackbirds, but then he stopped suddenly and took the flute out of his mouth.

'Do you know what I'm going to do tomorrow?' he said.

'Nope,' said Alfred. 'Is it some kind of mischief?'

Emil put his flute back in his mouth and began to play again. He walked along blowing for a while and thinking hard.

'I don't know,' he said at last. 'I never do know until afterwards.'

Enjoy Emil's
Sneaky Rat?

Turn the page for
a taste of another
of Emil's hilarious
adventures!

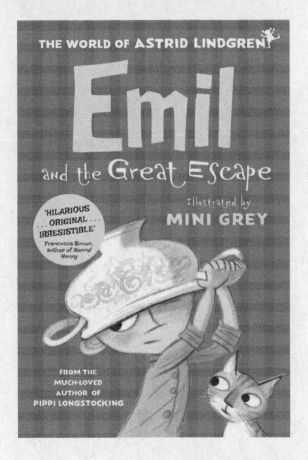

Whether he's running his little sister up a flagpole, or trying to escape after getting locked in a shed, Emil's adventures never stop. Hens, dogs, little sisters—and adults—all flee his path.

But Emil doesn't mean to be bad, it's just that trouble—and fun—follow him wherever he goes.

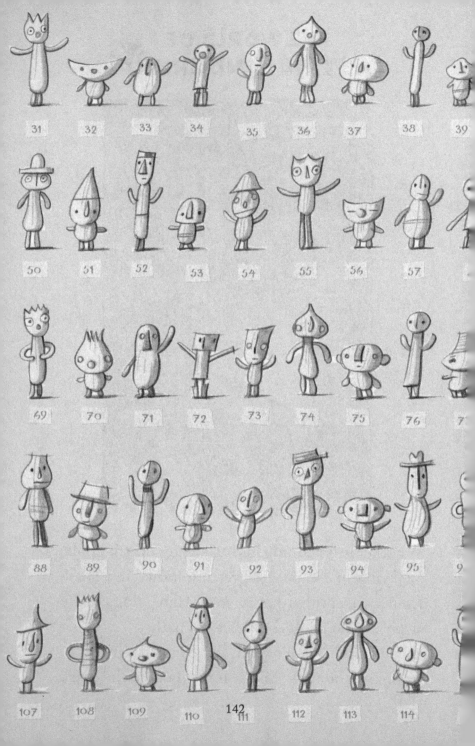

31   32   33   34   35   36   37   38   39

50   51   52   53   54   55   56   57

69   70   71   72   73   74   75   76   7

88   89   90   91   92   93   94   95   9

107   108   109   110   111   112   113   114

142

Once upon a time there was a boy called Emil, who lived in Lönneberga. He was a harum-scarum, stubborn little chap, not as nice as *you*, of course, but he *looked* nice enough, that is to say when he wasn't screaming. He had round blue eyes, a round, apple-cheeked face, and a mop of fair hair. In fact he often looked so nice that people might have thought he was a perfect little angel. But they would have been quite wrong. He was five years old and as strong as a young ox, and he lived at Katthult, in Lönneberga, a village in Småland, in Sweden.

One day his father went to town and bought him a cap. Emil was delighted with this cap, and wanted to wear it when he went to bed.

His mother wanted to hang it on a peg in the hall, but Emil yelled so that you could have heard him all over Lönneberga. And he slept with his cap on for nearly three weeks. It was one of those with a shiny black peak and a blue crown, and really did feel rather bumpy. But the great thing was that he had got his own way, that was the point.

One Christmas his mother tried to get him to eat some greens, as greens are so good for you, but Emil said no.

'Won't you eat *any* greens?' asked his mother.

'Yes,' said Emil. '*Real* greens.' And he sat quietly down behind the Christmas tree and started chewing it. But he soon tired of that because it scratched his mouth.

Well, that shows how stubborn Emil was. He wanted to boss his father and mother and the entire household, in fact the whole of Lönneberga itself, but the Lönnebergans weren't going to put up with that.

'I pity the folk up at Katthult, having such a badly-behaved boy. They'll never make anything of him,' they said.

Yes, that's what they thought! But they wouldn't have said so if they had known how Emil was going to turn out. Fancy if they had known he was going to be president of the local council when he grew up! You probably don't know what it means to be president of the local council, but I can assure you that it is something very grand, and that's what Emil was going to be, later on.

But just now we will talk about what happened when Emil was a little boy, living at Katthult in Småland, with his father, whose name was Anton Svensson, and his mother, whose name was Alma Svensson, and his little sister Ida. There was a farm lad, too, called Alfred, and a maidservant called Lina. Because when Emil was a little boy there were servants in Lönneberga and everywhere else. There were farmhands who ploughed and tended the horses and cattle and brought in the hay and planted potatoes, and maidservants who milked and washed up and scrubbed and sang to the children.

Now you know who lived in Katthult: father Anton, mother Alma, little Ida, Alfred, and Lina.

And there were two horses and a pair of oxen, eight cows, three pigs, ten sheep, fifteen hens, a cock, a cat, and a dog. And Emil.

Katthult was a lovely little farmstead, with a red-painted house on a hill and apple trees and lilac bushes all round it. And fields and ploughland and hedges and a lake and a great big wood.

It would have been quiet and peaceful in Katthult, but for Emil.

'He's always getting into mischief, that boy,' said Lina. 'And if he doesn't get into mischief on his own, something's always happening to him. I've never seen such a child.'

But Emil's mother stuck up for him.

'He's not so bad,' she said. 'Today he's only pinched Ida and spilt the cream for the coffee, that's all . . . oh yes, and chased the cat round the henhouse. I think he's beginning to behave better and growing less wild.'

And he wasn't really bad, nobody could call him that. He was very fond of Ida and the cat. But he had to pinch Ida to make her give him her bread and jam, and he chased the cat just in fun to see if he could run as fast as it could. Although the cat didn't realize this, of course.

It was on the seventh of March that Emil was so good and only pinched Ida and upset the cream and chased the cat. But now you shall hear about three other days in Emil's life, when other things happened, either because he got up to mischief, as Lina said, or because things always happened, wherever Emil was.

41 42 43 44 45 46 47 48

60 61 62 63 64 65 66 67

79 80 81 82 83 84 85 86

98 99 100 101 102 103 104 105

117 118 119 120 **149**121 122 123 124

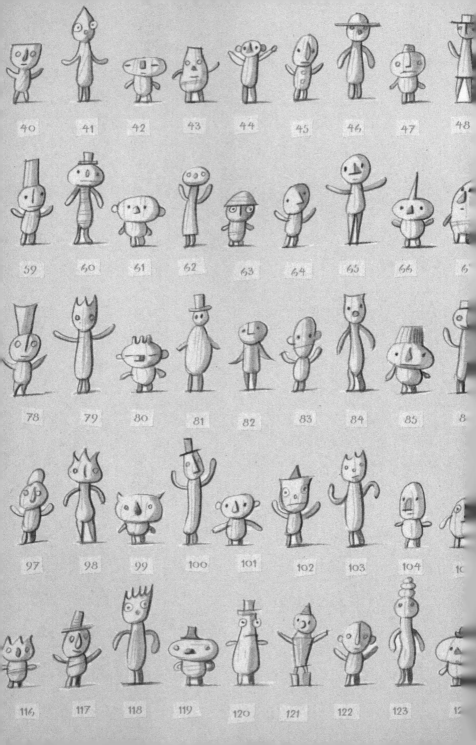

40 41 42 43 44 45 46 47 48

59 60 61 62 63 64 65 66 6

78 79 80 81 82 83 84 85 8

97 98 99 100 101 102 103 104 10

116 117 118 119 120 121 122 123 12

Be part of the fun that follows Emil everywhere he goes, as he teaches his pet pig to skip, puts a frog in the lunch basket, and paints his little sister blue—and that's just the start!

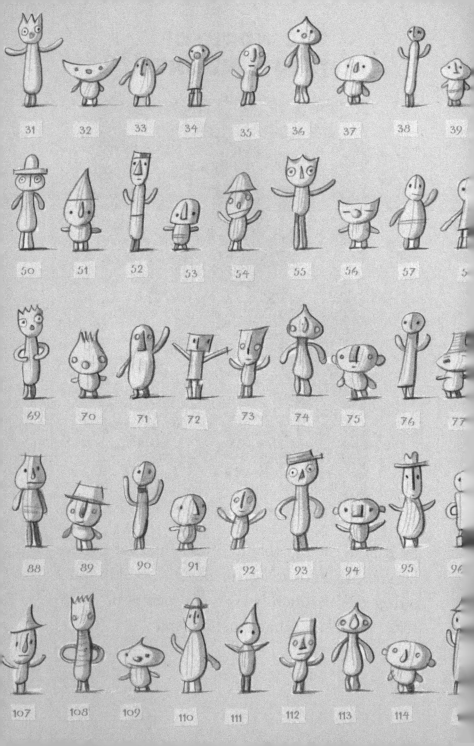

ABOUT THE AUTHOR

Astrid Lindgren was born in 1907, and grew up at a farm called Näs in the south of Sweden. Her first book was published in 1944, followed a year later by *Pippi Longstocking*. She wrote 34 chapter books and 41 picture books, that all together have sold 165 million copies worldwide. Her books have been translated into 107 different languages and according to UNESCO's annual list, she is the 18th most translated author in the world.

She created stories about Pippi, a free-spirited, red-haired girl to entertain her daughter, Karin, who was ill with pneumonia. The girl's name 'Pippi Longstocking' was in fact invented by Karin. Astrid Lindgren once commented about her work, 'I write to amuse the child within me, and can only hope that other children may have some fun that way, too.

For more information visit www.astridlindgren.com